Robert Lewis Weed

Adam Bede - A Play in Five Acts

Founded on George Eliot's Famous Novel

Robert Lewis Weed

Adam Bede - A Play in Five Acts
Founded on George Eliot's Famous Novel

ISBN/EAN: 9783337047610

Printed in Europe, USA, Canada, Australia, Japan

Cover: Foto ©Andreas Hilbeck / pixelio.de

More available books at **www.hansebooks.com**

Adam Bede

A PLAY IN FIVE ACTS

Founded on GEORGE ELIOT'S famous novel

BY

ROBERT LEWIS WEED

ACT FIRST.

SCENE FIRST—BROXTON, ENGLAND—THE RECTORY.

SCENE SECOND—HAYSLOPE, ENGLAND—THE HALL FARM.

ACT SECOND.

SCENE FIRST—(*Evening of next day*)—IN THE WOOD.

SCENE SECOND—(*One month later*)—THE CHASE LAWN.

ACT THIRD.

SCENE FIRST—(*Two days later*)—THE HERMITAGE.

SCENE SECOND—(*Next day*)—THE HALL FARM.

ACT FOURTH.

SCENE FIRST—BROXTON (*Eight months later*)—THE RECTORY.

SCENE SECOND—STONITON (*Two weeks later*)—THE PRISON.

ACT FIFTH.

INDIA, APRIL 6, 1799—(*Six months later*)—GROVE OF SULTANPÉT.

CAST OF CHARACTERS.

ADAM BEDE.
SQUIRE DONNITHORNE.
ARTHUR DONNITHORNE.
REVEREND ADOLPHUS IRWINE.
MARTIN POYSER.
SETH BEDE.
JOSHUA RANN.
MEESTER CRAIG.
MEESTER CASSON.
SURGEON MALTBY.
JACK CRANAGE.
FAYTHER TAFT.
FAYTHER POYSER.
BARTLE MASSEY.
CARROL (*a butler*).
MILLS (*a butler*).
MESSENGER.
JAILOR.
MRS. POYSER.
HETTY SORREL.
MRS. IRWINE.
LISBETH BEDE.
TOTTY POYSER.
MOLLY (*a maid*).
        AND
DINAH MORRIS.

Tenants, Farm-hands, Villagers, Soldiers, Sepoys.
Period—A. D. 1798-99.

ADAM BEDE.

ACT FIRST—SCENE FIRST.

THE RECTORY.   MORNING.   THE STUDY.

WINDOW R. DOOR L. C. LEADING INTO HALL; HALL-
STAIRS SEEN AT BACK. FIREPLACE L. WALLS LINED
WITH BOOKS. LARGE STUDY TABLE C. CHAIRS R. AND
L. ARMCHAIR AND HASSOCK NEAR FIRE L. SMALL
TABLE R. NEAR WINDOW, CHAIRS R. AND L. OF TABLE.

Discovered, MRS. IRWINE *and* REV. ADOLPHUS IR-
WINE *seated at small table* R. *playing chess.*

MRS. IRWINE—"There, Dauphin, tell me what that
is?" (*deposits her queen and quietly folds her arms.*)

REV. A. IRWINE—"Ah! you witch-mother, you sor-
ceress! How is a Christian man to win a game of you?
Before we began I should have sprinkled the board
with holy water. You've not won that game by fair
means, now, so don't pretend it!"

MRS. IRWINE—"Yes, yes, that's what the beaten
have always said of conquerors. Shall I give you another chance?"

Rev. Irwine—"No, mother, I shall leave you to your conscience." (*rises and looks out of window* R.) "The weather is clearing, we must go and splash up the mud a little, mustn't we, Juno?" (*strokes a brown setter affectionately.*)

Mrs. Irwine—"True, the sunshine is falling on the board to show more clearly what a foolish move you made with that pawn."

Rev. Irwine—"Mother, I'm ashamed of you! You are an ungenerous victor. But I must go upstairs and —" (*starts toward door; is met by* Carrol)

Enter Carrol (*door* L. C.)

Carroll—"If you please, sir, Joshua Rann wishes to speak with you."

Mrs. Irwine—"Let him be shown in here. I always like to hear what Mr. Rann has to say. His shoes will be dirty, but see that he wipes them, Carrol."

(*Exit* Carrol L. C.)

Mrs. Irwine—"What do you suppose can be the matter now, Dauphin?"

Rev. Irwine (*x's to fireplace*)—"I haven't the least idea, but something out of the ordinary you may be sure. Joshua is not the man to pay me a visit unless he has a grievance or some news to tell."

Enter Carrol L. C. *followed by* Joshua Rann.

Rev. Irwine—"Well, Joshua, good morning. Sit down."

Joshua Rann—"Thank your reverence, I'll stand if you please, as more becomin'." (*pulling a lock of his hair.*) "I hope I see your reverence well, an' Mrs. Irwine, well."

Rev. Irwine—"Yes, Joshua, thank you. You see how blooming my mother looks. She sets us younger

people an example in not giving way to age. (*dogs
sniff at* RANN'S *legs; he tries to be polite and not
notice them*) Never mind the dogs, Joshua, give them
a friendly kick. Here, Pug, you rascal. Is anything the
matter in Hayslope that you've come over this morning?"

JOSHUA—"Why, sir, I had to come to Brox'on to
deliver some work and I thought it 'ud be but right to
call an' let you know the goin's on as there's been i' the
village, such as I hanna seen i' my time, an' I've lived
in it man an' boy sixty year come Saint Thomas."

REV. IRWINE—"Well?"

JOSHUA—"I collected the Easter dues for Mr. Blink
afore your reverence come into the parish, an' been
at the ringin' o' ivery bell, an' the diggin' o' ivery
grave, an' sung i' the choir long afore Bartle Massey
come wi' his counter-singin' an' fine anthems as puts
iverybody out, but himself—one takin' it up after
another like sheep a-bleatin' i' the fold."

REV. IRWINE—"But, Joshua, you—"

JOSHUA—"I know what belongs to bein' a parish
clark, an' I know as I should be wantin i' respect to
your reverence, an' church, an' king, if I was t' allow
such goin's on wi'out speakin'."

REV. IRWINE—"Why, what in the world is the
matter, Joshua? Have the thieves been at the church
lead again?"

JOSHUA—"Thieves! no sir—an' yet, as I may say,
it is thieves, an' a-thievin' the church too. It's the
Methodisses as is like to get th' upper hand i' the parish, if your reverence, an' his honor Squire Donnithorne, doesna think well to say the word an' forbid it.
Not as I'm a-dictatin' to you, sir; I'm not forgettin'
myself so far as to be wise above my betters. Howiver,
whether I'm wise or no, what I've got to say, I say
—as sure as I'm a-standin' afore your reverence—the
young Methodist woman, Dinah Morris, as is at Meester Poyser's, ha' been a-preachin' an' a-prayin' on the
green."

REV. IRWINE—"Preaching on the green! What, that pale pretty young woman I've seen at Poyser's? I saw by her dress that she was a Methodist or a Quaker but I didn't know she was a preacher."

JOSHUA—"It's a true word as I say, sir; an' she preached there last night; an' she's laid hold o' Chad's Bess, so the gell's been i' fits welly iver sin'."

REV. IRWINE—"Well, Bessy Cranage is a hearty-looking lass; I dare say she'll come around again, Joshua. Did anybody else go into fits?" (looks at MRS. IRWINE amused)

JOSHUA—" No, sir—I canna say as they did. But there's no knowin' what'll come if we're t' ha' such preachin' as that a-goin on' ivery week; there'll be no livin' i' the village."

REV. IRWINE—"Well, what's your advice, Joshua? What do you think should be done?"

JOSHUA—"Your reverence, I'm not for takin' any measures agin' the young woman. She's Meester Poyser's own niece, and I donna wish to say what's any ways disrespectful o' th' family at th' Hall Farm, as I've measured for shoes little an' big, welly iver sin' I've been a shoemaker. She's well enough if she'd let preachin' alone; but Methodisses make folks believe as if they take a mug o' drink extra, an' make theirselves a bit comfortable, they'll have to go to hell for't, an' I make no doubt if th' young woman keeps on preachin' she'll stir other folks up to thinkin' th' same way. She ha' already got Will Maskery t' her way o' thinkin'."

REV. IRWINE—"Is Maskery preaching too?"

JOSHUA—"Nay, sir, he's no gift at stringin' th' words together wi'out th' book, but he's got tongue enough t' speak disrespectful aboot's neebors, an' what's worse, he's usin' the Bible t' find nicknames for folks as are his elders an' betters. I could bring them as 'ud swear as he called me 'a blind Pharisee,' an' you, forgi'e me for sayin' such things over agin', 'a dumb dog an' a idle Shepherd.'"

REV. IRWINE—"Let evil words die as soon as they are spoken, Joshua. If you can bring me any proof that Will Maskery annoys his neighbors or creates disturbance, I shall think it my duty as a clergyman and a magistrate, to interfere. But it wouldn't become wise people like you and me to make a fuss about trifles. We must live and let live, Joshua, in religion as well as in other things. You go on doing your duty as parish clerk and sexton as well as you've always done it, and making those capital thick boots for your neighbors, and things won't go far wrong in Hayslope, depend upon it."

JOSHUA—"Your reverence is good to say so; an' I'm sensible as you not livin' i' th' parish, there's more upo' my shoulders."

REV. IRWINE—"I shall trust to your good sense to take no notice of what Will Maskery says, either of you or of me." (*sits* R. *of table* C.) "When you've done your day's work, you can go on taking your pot of beer soberly, just as you have always done, and if Will Maskery doesn't want to join you, but prefers to go to a prayer-meeting on the green, why, let him; that is no business of yours, so long as he doesn't hinder you from doing what you like."

JOSHUA—"Ah, sir! But when he comes to church, an' we're a singin', he sits an' shakes his head, till I should like to fetch him a rap across the jowl.—God forgi'e me, an' Mrs. Irwine, an' your reverence, too, for speakin' so afore you—but he said as our Christmas singin' was no better nor th' cracklin' o' thorns under a pot."

REV. IRWINE—"It must be that he has no ear for music, Joshua. Never fear; he won't bring anyone else in Hayslope to his opinion."

JOSHUA—"Yes, sir; but it turns a man's stomach t' hear th' scripture misused i' that way. I know as much o' th' words o' th' Bible as he does, an' could say the Psalms right through i' my sleep, if you was to pinch me; but I know better nor to take such words t' say my own say wi'."

Rap at the door, voice heard calling out:

"Godson Arthur, may he come in?"

MRS. IRWINE—"Come in, come in, godson."

Enter ARTHUR DONNITHORNE L. C. *dressed in riding costume.*

MRS. IRWINE—"Ah, Arthur, welcome." (ARTHUR *kisses* MRS. IRWINE, *shakes hands with* REV. IRWINE.)
REV. IRWINE—"Glad to see you, Arthur, and where did you drop from?"
ARTHUR—"From the Chase." (*sits on edge of table* c.) "I couldn't stand being shut in the house a moment longer; as soon as the rain stopped I ordered my horse for a canter. The roads are a bit heavy but, (*turning for a chair sees* JOSHUA)—don't let me interrupt Joshua's business—he has something to say."
JOSHUA—"Belike sir, you hanna heard as Thias Bede's took to drinkin' bad again. If your reverence sees well and good, I hope you'll go an' labor wi' Thias, fur he's a dreadful sinner. He's a-slippin' away, fast."
REV. IRWINE—"To be sure, Joshua, to be sure. I'll try and do what I can for him. And now good-morning, Joshua; go into the kitchen and have some ale."
JOSHUA—"Thank your reverence. Good mornin', Mrs. Irwine, good mornin', Captain Donnithorne, good mornin', your reverence." (*exit* JOSHUA L. C.)
REV. IRWINE—"Poor old Thias. It's a pity that Adam should have this cross added to the load already on his shoulders. For the last five years he has been propping up his father from ruin."
ARTHUR—"Adam Bede is a trump!" (*x's to fire*) "When I was a little fellow and Adam a strapping lad

of fifteen he taught me carpentering, and I used to think if ever I was a rich Sultan, I would make Adam my grand vizier."

REV. IRWINE—"And I believe he would stand the exaltation as well as any poor wiseman in an eastern story."

ARTHUR—"If ever I live to be a large-acred man, instead of a poor devil with a mortgaged allowance of pocket money, I'll have Adam for my right hand. He shall manage my woods for me. He seems to have a better notion of those things than any man I ever met. I'm trying to persuade my grandfather to engage Adam in place of that miserable old Satchell, who understands no more about timber than an old carp. But come, your reverence. (*x's to table* C.) Are you for a ride with me? I want to call at the Hall Farm to look at the whelps Poyser is keeping for me."

MRS. IRWINE—"You must stay and have a glass of wine first, Arthur. Carrol will bring it in directly."

REV. IRWINE—"Yes, I want to go to the Hall Farm, too, I have some curiosity to have another look at Dinah Morris, the little Methodist who is staying there. Joshua tells me she was preaching on the green last night."

ARTHUR—"Oh, by Jove! was that Dinah Morris? I happened to be riding past and saw her. She looked like Saint Catherine in a Quaker dress. It's a type of face one rarely sees among our common people. (*sits* L. *of table* C.)

MRS. IRWINE—"If she is so attractive, I should like to see the young woman, Dauphin. Make her come here, on some pretext or other."

REV. IRWINE—"I don't see how I can manage that, mother; it will hardly do for me, a church of England clergyman, to patronize a Methodist preacher. Besides, I doubt if she would consent to be patronized by an 'idle shepherd.'"

MRS. IRWINE—"You should have come in a little

sooner, Arthur, to hear Joshua's denunciation of his neighbor, Will Maskery."

REV. IRWINE—"Yes, the old fellow wants me to ex-communicate the wheelwright and then deliver him over to the Civil arm—that is to say, to your grand-father,—to be turned out of house and yard."

MRS. IRWINE—"It is really insolent of the man, though, to call you an 'idle shepherd and a dumb dog.' I should be inclined to check him a little. You're too easy-tempered, Dauphin."

REV. IRWINE—"Why, mother, I'm not sure but he is right about it. I am a lazy fellow."

MRS. IRWINE—"Tut, tut, Dauphin."

REV. IRWINE—"Oh, but there's truth in it, mother. You can use your right arm quite well now, Arthur?"

ARTHUR—"Yes, pretty well; but the doctor insists upon my keeping it up constantly for some time to come. Though I hope I shall be able to get away to the regiment in the beginning of August. It's a des-perately dull business being shut up at the Chase when one can neither hunt nor fish. However, we are to astonish the echoes on the 30th, when I come of age. Grandfather has given me carte blanche for once, and I promise you the entertainment shall be worthy of the occasion. I think I shall have a lofty throne built for you, godmother, (*x's to* MRS. IRWINE *and stands by her chair*) so that you may sit and look down upon us like an Olympian goddess."

MRS. IRWINE—"And I mean to grace the occasion and bring out my best brocade that I wore at your christening twenty years ago. Ah, Arthur, (*takes his hand and holds it*) I think I see your poor mother flitting about in her white dress, which looked to me that very day almost like a shroud; and it was her shroud only three months after; and your little cap and christening dress were buried with her. She had set her heart on that, sweet soul. Arthur, thank God you take after your mother's family. If you had been a puny, yellow baby, I wouldn't have stood godmother to you."

Rev. Irwine—"But you might have been a little too hasty, there, mother. Don't you remember how it was with Juno's last pups? One of them was the very image of its mother, but it has two or three of its father's tricks notwithstanding. Nature is clever enough to cheat even you, mother."

Mrs. Irwine—"Nonsense, child. Nature never makes a ferret in the shape of a mastiff. You'll never persuade me that I can't tell what men are by their outsides. If I don't like a man's looks depend upon it I shall never like him. I don't want to know people that look ugly any more than I want to taste dishes that look disagreeable. If at the first glance they make me shudder, I say take them away. An ugly, fishy eye makes me feel quite ill, it's like a bad smell."

Arthur—"Talking of eyes, reminds me that I have a book of poems I meant to bring you, godmother. 'The Ancient Mariner,' attracted me most, but I can hardly make head or tail of it as a story, it's a strange, striking thing. I'll send it over to you. By the way, your reverence, (*x's to table* c.) in a parcel that came down from London I found some pamphlets about Antinomianism and Evangelicalism, whatever they may be, would you like to have them?"

Rev. Irwine—"I don't know that I'm very fond of 'isms,' but I may as well look at the pamphlets, they let one see what is going on. If you had stuck to your books, you rascal, you would enjoy talking these things over with me."

Mrs. Irwine—"Dauphin, Dauphin, you mustn't be severe with Arthur."

Arthur—"Quite right, godmother, his reverence forgets that scholarship doesn't run in my family. I shall be satisfied if I remember enough Latin to adorn my maiden speech in Parliament."

Rev. Irwine—"Arthur!"

Arthur—"Will your reverence kindly tell me what

need a country gentleman has for knowledge of the classics? To my thinking, he would much better have a knowledge of fertilizers."

MRS. IRWINE—"Godson Arthur! Reflect, what are you saying?"

ARTHUR—"Don't be alarmed, godmother, I've only come to the conclusion that I should like to help the farmers in a better management of their lands. Take the Stonyshire side of the estate,—it's in a dismal condition—now I should like to set improvements on foot, and gallop about from place to place and overlook them. Know all the laborers and see them touching their hats to me with a look of good will."

REV. IRWINE—"Bravo, Arthur! You may not care for the classics, but you atone for that if you help raise the food required by those who do appreciate them. When you enter upon your career of model landlord, may I be there to see it." (*rising.*)

MRS. IRWINE—"And when that day comes, mind, you fall in love with the right person; for if you get a wife who drains your purse, she'll make you niggardly in spite of yourself."

ARTHUR—"Never fear, godmother, about my marrying while my grandfather lives. But come, your reverence, are you ready to start for the Hall Farm?"

REV. IRWINE—"In one moment, I've a little matter to attend to, and then I'll be ready to set out with you." (*exit* REV. IRWINE L. C.)

ARTHUR—"Speaking of the Hall Farm. Have you seen Poyser's niece, Hetty Sorrel, godmother?" (*sits R. of table* C.)

MRS. IRWINE—"No, I don't remember that I have, is she pretty?"

Enter CARROL L. C. *with wine, passes it to each and exits.*

ARTHUR—"Pretty! she's a perfect Hebe; if I were an artist I would paint her." (*strikes his boot with his whip.*)

Mrs. Irwine—"Why, Arthur, you are enthusiastic. You are quite sure that she appeals to you only in an artistic light?"

Arthur—"What do you mean, godmother?"

Mrs. Irwine—"I mean you mustn't fill her little head with the notion that she's attractive to fine gentlemen, else you will spoil her for a poor man's wife."

Voice of Rev. Irwine *heard outside calling.*

Rev. Irwine—"I'm ready, Arthur, the horses are at the door."

Arthur—"All right, your reverence. Good-bye, godmother." (*kisses her.*)

Mrs. Irwine—"Come again soon, Arthur."

Arthur—"Yes, Godmother." (*going to door.*)

Mrs. Irwine—"Arthur! (*calling him back*) mind what I say, don't feed the girl's vanity."

Arthur—"Never fear, godmother, never fear. Good-bye."

End of scene first, act first.

ACT FIRST—SCENE SECOND.

The Hall Farm. Early Afternoon. The Kitchen.

The Kitchen.

Garden door upper r. outside door r. c. dairy door l. c. Door leading into front part of house l. Armchair by fire r. Cupboard at back between doors r. c. and l. c. Table l. Chairs r. and l. Ironing board resting on two chairs r. Bowl of starch standing on the end of ironing board l. Tub of whey seen standing in dairy-way l. c.

Discovered, MRS. POYSER *ironing* R. TOTTY *seated in a high chair at the end of ironing table with a miniature iron.* MOLLY *sweeping* L.

TOTTY—"Munny, my iron's twite told; pease put it down to warm."

MRS. POYSER—"Cold is it, my darling? Bless your sweet face." (*kisses the child.*) "Never mind, mother's done her ironing now. She's going to put the ironing things away."

TOTTY—"Munny, I tould ike to doo into de barn to Tommy."

MRS. POYSER—"No, no, Totty 'ud get her feet wet. Run into the dairy and see cousin Hetty make the butter."

TOTTY—"I tould ike a bit o' pum-take." (MRS. POYSER *turns away toward the fire.* TOTTY *upsets the bowl of starch on the ironing board.*) "Oh, Munny, I'se spilted de starch."

MRS. POYSER—"Did anybody iver see the like? (*running towards the table.*) The child's allays i' mischief if your back's turned a minute. What shall I do to you, you naughty, naughty gell?"

TOTTY *exits hastily into the dairy* L. C. MRS. POYSER *wipes up the starch.*

MOLLY—"I've finished sweeping ma'am, shall I go out to the barn and comb the wool for the whittaws till milking time?"

MRS. POYSER—"Comb the wool for the whittaws! That's what you'd like to be doing is it? To think of a gell o' your age a-wanting to go and sit wi' half a dozen men!"

MOLLY—"I'm sure I donna want t' go wi' th' whittaws, on'y we allays used to comb th' wool for'n at Master Ottley's; an' so I just axed ye."

MRS. POYSER—"Master Ottley's, indeed! It's fine talking o' what you did at Mr. Ottley's—and you know no more o' what belongs to work when you come here, than the mawkin i' the field. And what are you standin' there for like a jack as is run down instead o' gettin' your wheel out?" (MOLLY *goes towards door* L.)

Enter DINAH MORRIS L. MOLLY *stands aside for* DINAH *to enter, then exits door* L.

DINAH—"Don't be so hard on the girl, aunt,—she means to do right." (*x's to* C.)

MRS. POYSER—"Means to do right! She's as poor a two-fisted thing as ever I saw. My goodness, Dinah, (*x's to* DINAH C.) how you do look the image o' your Aunt Judith. I could almost fancy it was thirty years ago, and I was a little gell at home looking at Judith as she sat at her work. Judith and me allays hung together, though she had such queer ways, but your mother and her never could agree. Your mother little thought as she'd have a daughter just cut out after the very pattern o' Judith, and leave her an orphan for Judith to take care on and bring up wi' a spoon when she was in the graveyard. I allays said that o' Judith, as she'd bear a pound weight any day, to save anybody else carrying a ounce."

DINAH—"She was a blessed woman."

MRS. POYSER—"She was just the same from the first o' my remembering her; it made no difference in her as I could see, when she took to the Methodists. Only she talked a bit different and wore a different sort o' cap."

DINAH—"And she was very fond of you, too, Aunt Rachel, (*sits in chair* L. *of table* L.) I've often heard her talk of you in a loving way. (*takes up sheet from table and begins sewing.*) When she had that bad illness and I was only eleven years old, she used to say, 'If I'm taken away, Dinah, you'll find a friend in your Aunt Rachel, for she has a kind heart,' and I'm sure I've found it so."

Mrs. Poyser—"I don't know how a body could be anything but kind to you, Dinah. (*putting away ironing board* UPPER L. *corner*) You know I'd ha' been glad to behave to you like a mother's sister if you'd come and live wi' us. Then you might get married to Seth Bede, and though he is a poor wool-gathering Methodist, as is never like to have a penny beforehand, I know your uncle 'ud help you with a pig, and very like a cow, for he'd do as much for you as he'd do for Hetty, though she's his own niece. And there's linen in the house as I could well spare you. There's a piece o' sheeting I could give you as that squinting Kitty spun,—she was a rare girl to spin, for all she squinted and the children couldn't abide her,—but where's the use o' talkin', if you wonna be persuaded to settle down i'stead o' wearin' yourself out wi' walking and preaching and givin' away every penny you get, so as you've got notions i' your head about religion more nor what's i' the Catechism and the Prayerbook."

Dinah—"But not more than what's in the Bible, aunt."

Mrs. Poyser—"Yes, and the Bible, too, for that matter. Else why shouldn't them as know best what's in the Bible,—the parsons and the people as have nothing to do but learn it the same as you do? But for th' matter o' that, if everybody was to do like you, the world must come to a standstill, for if we're to despise th' things o' this world, as you say, I should like to know where th' pick o' th' stock an' th' corn an' th' best milk cheeses 'ud have to go? Everybody 'ud be wantin' bread made o' tail-ends, an' everybody 'ud be runnin' after everybody else to preach to 'em, i'stead o' bringin' up their families an' layin' by against a bad harvest."

Dinah—"Nay, dear aunt, you never heard me say that all people are called to forsake their work and their families. It's quite right the land should be plowed and sowed, and the precious corn stored and the things of this life cared for, and right that people should rejoice in their families, and care for them. We are all servants of God wherever our lot is cast, but He gives us different kinds of work according as He fits us for it. I can no more help spending my life in trying to help others, than you can help running when you hear little Totty crying at the other end of the house."

MRS. POYSER—"Ah, I know it 'ud be just th' same if I was to talk to you for hours. You'd make me th' same answer at th' end. I might as well talk to th' running brook an' tell it to stan' still. (*looking out the door* R. C.) If there is'nt Captain Donnithorne an' Mr. Irwine a-coming into th' yard. I'll lay my life they're comin' to speak about your preachin' on the green; Dinah, it's you must answer 'em for I'm dumb! I've said enough a'ready about your bringing such disgrace upo' your uncle's family. I wouldn't ha' minded if you'd been Poyser's own niece; folks must put up wi' their own kin as they put up wi' their own noses— it's their own flesh an' blood. But to think of a niece o' mine being cause o' my husband's being turned out o' his farm and me brought him no fortin' but my savin's—"

DINAH—"Nay, Aunt Rachel, you have no cause for such fears. I've strong assurance that no evil will happen to you and my uncle and the children, from anything I've done. I didn't preach without direction."

MRS. POYSER—"Direction! I know what you mean by direction. When there's a bigger maggot than usual in your head you call it direction, and then nothing can stir you. I canna ha' common patience wi' you." (*advances to the door* R. C. *courtesying.*)

Enter MR. IRWINE *and* CAPTAIN DONNITHORNE, R. C.

REV. IRWINE—"Well, Mrs. Poyser, how are you after this stormy morning? Our feet are quite dry; we shall not soil your beautiful floor."

Mrs. Poyser—"O, sir, don't mention it. Will you and the captain please to walk into the parlor?"

Arthur—"No, indeed, thank you, Mrs. Poyser, I delight in your kitchen, I think it's the most charming room I know. I should like every farmer's wife to come and look at it for a pattern."

Mrs. Poyser—"Oh, you're pleased to say so, sir; pray, take a seat."

Arthur—"Is Poyser at home?"

Mrs. Poyser—"No, sir, he isn't, he's gone to Rossiter to see Mr. West, the factor, about the wool. But there's father in the barn, sir, if he'd be of any use?"

Arthur—"No, thank you; I'll just look at the whelps and leave a message about them with your shepherd. I must come another day and see your husband. Do you know when he's likely to be at home?"

Mrs. Poyser—"Why, sir, you can hardly miss him except on market-day,—that's of a Friday, you know; for if he's anywhere on the farm, we can send for him in a minute. If we'd got rid o' th' Scantlands we should have no outlying fields; an' I should be glad of it, for if iver anything happens, he's sure to be gone to the Scantlands. Things allays happens so contrary if they've a chance; and it's an unnat'ral thing to ha' one bit o' your farm in one county and all the rest in another."

Arthur—"Yes, the Scantlands would go much better with Choyce's farm, especially as he wants dairy land and you've got plenty. But do you know. Mrs. Poyser, I think your farm is the prettiest on the estate, and if I were going to marry and settle down I should be tempted to turn you out and run the Hall Farm, myself."

Mrs. Poyser—"O, sir, you wouldn't like it at all. As for farmin' it's puttin' money into your pocket wi' your right hand and fetchin' it out wi' your left. As fur as I can see, it's raisin' victuals for other folks, and just gettin' a mouthful for yourself and your children as you go along. Not as you'd be like a poor man as wants to get his bread; for you could afford to lose as much money as you liked wi' farmin', but it's poor fun losing money; though I understand it's what the great folks o' London play at moie than anything else. But you know more about that than I do, sir. As for farmin', sir, I canna think as you'd like it; and this house—the draughts in it are enough to cut you through, and it's my opinion the floors upstairs are very rotten."

Arthur—"Why, that's a terrible picture, Mrs. Poyser, I think I should be doing you a favor to turn you out of such a place. But there's no chance of that. I'm not likely to settle down for the next twenty years, till I'm a stout gentleman of forty; and my grandfather would never consent to part with such good tenants as you and Poyser."

Mrs. Poyser—"Well, sir, if your grandfather thinks so well of Mr. Poyser for a tenant I wish you'd put in a word for him to allow us some new gates for the Five Closes. My husband's been askin' an' askin' till he's tired; an' to think o' what he's' done for the farm and never's had a penny allowed him, be the times bad or good. But as I've said to my husband often an' often, I'm sure if the captain had anything to do with it, it wouldn't be so. Not as I wish to speak disrespectful o' them as have got th' power i' their hands, but it's more than flesh and blood 'ull bear sometimes, to be toiling an' strivin', up early an' down late, an' hardly sleepin' a wink for thinkin' as the cheese may swell, or the wheat may grow green again i' th' sheaf; an' arter all, at th' end o' th' year to be no better off, than if you'd been cookin' a feast an' had got th' smell o' it for your pains."

Arthur—"I'm afraid I should only do harm instead of good if I were to speak about the gates, Mrs. Poyser, though I assure you there's no man on the estate I would sooner say a word for than your husband. I know his farm is in better order than any other within ten miles of us; and as for the kitchen, I don't believe there's one in the kingdom to beat it. (*Hetty's laugh heard in the dairy* L. c.) By the bye, I've never seen your dairy; I must see your dairy, Mrs. Poyser."

MRS. POYSER—"Indeed, sir, it isn't fit for you to go into, for Hetty's in the middle o' makin' the butter, for the churning was thrown late an' I'm quite ashamed."

ARTHUR—"Oh, I've no doubt it's in capital order. Take me in." (ARTHUR *leads the way into the dairy* L. c. MRS. POYSER *follows expostulating.*)

(MR. IRWINE *advances toward* DINAH L., *who rises from chair.*)

REV. IRWINE—"You are only a visitor in this neighborhood, I think?" (*motions* DINAH *to resume her seat. He sits opposite her at table* L.)

DINAH—"Yea, sir, I come from Snowfield, in Stonyshire. I'd been ill and my aunt was very kind wanting me to have a rest from my work there, and invited me to come and stay with her awhile."

REV. IRWINE—"Ah, I remember Snowfield very well; to my thinking it's a dreary, bleak place. I once had occasion to go there; at that time they were building a cotton mill; but that's many years ago, now I suppose the place is a good deal changed."

DINAH—"It is changed, sir, for the mill has brought many people there to get a livelihood. I work in it myself and have reason to be grateful, for thereby I have enough and to spare. But it is a bleak place as you say, sir,—very different from this country."

REV. IRWINE—"You have relatives living there, probably, so that you are attached to the place as your home?"

DINAH—"I had an aunt there once who brought me up. She was taken away seven years ago, and I have no other kindred that I know of, besides my Aunt Poyser, who would have me come and live in this country,—but I'm not free to leave Snowfield, for there I was first planted, and have grown deep into it like the small grass on the hill-top."

REV. IRWINE—"Ah, I dare say, you have many religious friends and companions there; you are a Methodist, a Wesleyan, I think?"

DINAH—"Yea, my aunt at Snowfield belonged to the society."

REV. IRWINE—"And have you been long in the habit of preaching?—for I understand you preached at Hayslope last night."

DINAH—"I first took to the work four years since."

REV. IRWINE—"Women's preaching is sanctioned then, by your society?"

DINAH—"It doesn't forbid them, sir, when they've a clear call to the work. Mrs. Fletcher, as you may have heard about, was the first woman to preach in the society, and Mr. Wesley approved of her undertaking the work, for she had a great gift. There are many other women now who are helpers in the work, though I understand of late there's been voices raised against it in the society. I cannot but think their counsel will come to naught. It isn't for men to make channels for God's spirit as they make channels for the water courses, and say, flow here, but flow not there."

REV. IRWINE—"But tell me, if I may ask, how you first came to think of preaching."

DINAH—"Indeed, sir, I didn't think of it at all. I was led like a child, by a way that it knows not."

REV. IRWINE—"Tell me the circumstances, just how it was, the very day you began to preach."

DINAH—"It was one Sunday, and I walked with Brother Marlow, an aged preacher, to a village where there are lead mines and where the people live like sheep without a shepherd. It was summer time, and as we walked over the hills, I had a wonderful sense of the Divine Love. There are no trees there, you know, sir, and the heavens were stretched out like a tent and I felt the everlasting arms about me. It was a long walk, and when we got to the village Brother

Marlow was seized with a dizziness that forced him to lie down and he couldn"t stand up to preach. So I went to tell the people, thinking we'd go into one of the houses and I would read and pray with them. But as I passed the cottages and saw the aged, trembling women and the hard looks of the men who seemed to have their eyes no more filled with the sight of the Sabbath morning than if they had been dumb oxen, I felt a great movement in my soul and I trembled as if I was shaken by a strong spirit. I went to where the little flock of people was gathered together and stepped on the low wall that was built against the green hillside, and I spoke the words that were given to me. They all came round me, and many wept over their sins and have since been joined to the Lord. This was the beginning of my preaching, sir, and I've preached ever since." (*she stoops and gathers up her sewing.*)

REV. IRWINE—"And what did you think of your hearers last night? Did you find them quiet and attentive?"

DINAH—"Very quiet, sir. But I saw no signs of any great work upon them."

REV. IRWINE—"Our farm laborers are not easily roused. They take life slowly. But we have some intelligent workmen about here, the Bedes, for instance. By the by, Seth Bede is a Methodist."

DINAH—"Yea, I know Seth well, and his brother Adam, a little. Seth is a gracious young man, sincere and without offense. And Adam is like the patriarch Joseph, for his great skill and the kindness he shows to his brother and parents."

Enter ARTHUR DONNITHORNE, MRS. POYSER *and* HETTY SORREL L. C.

REV. IRWINE (*giving his hand to* DINAH)—"Goodbye. I hear you are going away soon; but this will not be the last visit you will pay your aunt,—so we shall meet again, I hope." (*x's to* R.)

ARTHUR—"I hope you will be ready for a great holiday on the 30th, Mrs. Poyser. You know what is to happen then, and I shall expect you to be one of the guests who come earliest and stay latest. Will you promise me your hand for two dances, Miss Hetty? If I don't get your promise now, I know I shall hardly have a chance, for all the smart young farmers will take care to secure you."

MRS. POYSER—"Indeed, sir, you're very kind to take that notice of her. An' I'm sure wheniver you're pleased to dance wi' her, she'll be proud an' thankful, if she stood still all the rest o' th' evening."

ARTHUR—"Oh, no, no, that would be too cruel to all the other young fellows who can dance. But you will promise me two dances, won't you?"

HETTY—(*courtesying with a coquettish glance*) "Yes, thank you, sir."

ARTHUR—"And you must bring all your children, you know, Mrs. Poyser; your little Totty as well as the boys. I want all the youngest children on the estate to be there; all those who will be fine young men and women when I'm a bald old fellow."

MRS. POYSER—"Oh, dear sir, that'll be a long time first."

ARTHUR—"But where is Totty to-day? I want to see her."

MRS. POYSER—"Where is the little 'un, Hetty?"

HETTY—"I don't know. She went into the brew house to Molly, I think."

MRS. POYSER *exits hastily* L. C. *going* L. ARTHUR *and* HETTY *talk aside.* REV. IRWINE *x's back and speaks again with* DINAH L.

ARTHUR—"And do you carry the butter to market when you've made it?"

HETTY—"Oh, no, sir, not when it's so heavy; I'm not strong enough. Alick takes it on horseback."

ARTHUR—"No, I'm sure your pretty arms were

never meant for such heavy weights. But you go out walking sometimes these pleasant evenings, don't you? Why don't you have a walk in the Chase grounds, now they are so green and pleasant? I hardly ever see you anywhere except at church."

HETTY—"Aunt doesn't like me to go a-walking alone. But I go through the Chase sometimes."

ARTHUR—"You go to see Mrs. Best the house-keeper?"

HETTY—"No, it isn't Mrs. Best, it's Mrs. Pomfret, the lady's-maid."

ARTHUR—"Ah, yes, yes, I knew I'd seen you at the Chase. She's teaching you something?"

HETTY—"Yes, sir, the lace mending as she learned abroad, and the stocking mending—"

ARTHUR—"Do you come every week to see Mrs. Pomfret?"

HETTY—"Yes, sir, every Thursday."

ARTHUR—"What time does Mrs. Pomfret expect you?"

HETTY—"Four o'clock sir, because that gives us time before Miss Donnithorne's bell rings."

ARTHUR—"And do you always go up the beach avenue?"

HETTY—"Most always, sir."

ARTHUR—"You'll be likely to next Thursday?"

HETTY—"Yes, sir."

ARTHUR—"To-morrow I'm going to Eagledale for a day's fishing, but I shall be back by Thursday."

Enter MRS. POYSER *with* TOTTY L. C. MR. IRWINE *x's to door* R. C. *and stands waiting for* ARTHUR.

MRS. POYSER—"Here she is, sir." (*leads* TOTTY *to* ARTHUR.)

ARTHUR—"Well, well. (*lifts the child and sets her on the arm of the arm chair* R. *holds on to her*) as I live. What a fine child she is. By the way what's her other name? She wasn't christened Totty?"

MRS. POYSER—"O, sir, we call her sadly out o' her name. Charlotte's her Christian name. We began by calling her Lotty, and now it's got to be Totty. To be sure it's more like a name for a dog than a Christian child."

ARTHUR—"Oh, no, Totty's a capital name. Why she looks like a Totty. Has she got a pocket on? (TOTTY *lifts her apron and shows empty pocket.*)

TOTTY—"I dot notin' in it."

ARTHUR—"No? What a pity! such a pretty pocket. Well I think I've got something in mine that will make a pretty jingle in yours. Yes, I declare I've got five little round silver things, and hear what a pretty noise they make in Totty's pink pocket." (TOTTY *smiles, then jumps down and goes to* HETTY *to have her hear the jingle.*)

MRS. POYSER—"Oh, for. shame, you naughty gell! Not to thank the captain for what he's given you. I'm sure it's very kind of you, but she's spoiled shameful, her father won't say her nay in anything, an' there's no managing her. It's being the youngest, an' th' only gell, sir."

ARTHUR—"Don't apologize. she's a nice little chick. I wouldn't have her different. But I must be going, the rector is waiting for me."

MRS. POYSER (*to* REV. IRWINE)—"I've never asked after Mrs. Irwine and the Misses Irwine. I hope they're as well as usual, sir?"

REV. IRWINE—"Yes, thank you. Mrs. Poyser, except that Miss Annie has one of her bad headaches to-day. Let me thank you for that nice cream cheese you sent us. My mother enjoyed it especially."

MRS. POYSER—"I'm very glad, indeed, sir. It's but seldom I make one, but I remembered Mrs. Irwine was fond of 'em. Please to give my duty to her and to Miss Kate and to Miss Annie." (*courtesies*)

REV. IRWINE—"Thank you—good-bye."

ARTHUR—"Just ride on slowly, Irwine, I'll overtake you. (*exit* REV. IRWINE R. C.) I want to speak to

the shepherd about the whelps. Good-bye, Mrs. Poyser, tell your husband I shall come and have a long
talk with him soon." (*exit* ARTHUR R. C.)

Exit HETTY *and* TOTTY *into garden* UPPER R. MRS.
POYSER *courtesies and watches visitors from door.*

MRS. POYSER—"Mr. Irwine wasn't angry then?
What did he say to you, Dinah? Didn't he scold you
for preachin'?"

DINAH—"No, he was very friendly. I was quite
drawn out to speak to him. His countenance is as
pleasant as the morning sunshine."

MRS. POYSER—"Pleasant! And what else did y' expect to find him, but pleasant? It's summat like to
see such a man as that i' the desk of a Sunday. As I
say to Poyser, he's like a good meal o' victual—you're
the better for him wi'out thinkin' on't. (*x's to* DINAH
L.)   But what did Mr. Irwine say to you about
preachin' on the green?"

DINAH—"He only said he'd heard of it; he didn't
seem to feel any displeasure about it. But, dear aunt,
don't think any more about that. (*laying aside work*)
He told me something that will cause you sorrow as
it does me. Thias Bede has taken to drink again. I'm
thinking the aged mother may be in need of comfort.
Perhaps I can be of use to her." (*rises*)

MRS. POYSER—"Dear heart, I'm quite willing you
should go an' see th' old woman, for you're one
as is allays welcome in trouble, Methodist or no
Methodist, but for th' matter o' that it's th' flesh an'
blood folks are made on as makes th' difference. Some
cheeses are made o' skimmed milk an' some o' new milk
an' it's no matter what you call 'em, you may tell
which is which by th' look an' th' smell. As for Thias
Bede, he'd be better out o' the way nor in it."

DINAH—"Nay, aunt, we must not judge." (*exit
door* L.)

MRS. POYSER—(*looking out of the door* R. C.) "There

·comes Poyser wi' gardener Craig. Poyser seems mighty fond of Craig; but for my part I think he's welly like a cock as thinks th' sun's rose o' purpose t' hear him crow."

Enter MR. POYSER *and* CRAIG R. C. *They stand in the door a moment and look out.*

CRAIG—"Well, Meester Poyser, ye'll not be carrying your hay to-morrow I'm thinkin'; ye may rely upo' my word as we'll ha' more downfall afore twenty-four hours is past. Ye see that darkish-blue cloud there upo' th' 'rizon—you know what I mean by th' 'rizon? where th' land an' sky seems t' meet?"

POYSER—"Aye, aye, I see the cloud."

CRAIG—"Well, you mark my words, as that cloud 'ull spread o'er th' hull sky soon. It's a great thing to ha' studied th' look o' th' clouds. Lord bless you! th' met'orological almanacs can learn me nothing, but there's a plenty o' things I could let them up to if they'd just come to me. (*coming down* C.) An' how are you, Mrs. Poyser?"

MRS. POYSER—"As well as could be expected, Mr. Craig. Poyser, you just missed Captain Donnithorne an' Mr. Irwine, as called askin' for you."

POYSER—"Did the captain leave any word?"

MRS. POYSER—"Yes, he said to tell you as he'd call again soon t' ha' a long talk wi' you."

CRAIG—"Ah, there's a mon for you as is a mon! Wi' such as Captain Arthur i' the army, a mon doesna need t' see fur to know as th' English 'ull beat the French. I know a mon as his father had a particular knowledge o' th' French, an' he says upo' good authority, as it's a big Frenchmon as reaches five feet high, for they live upo' spoon-meat mostly. An wi' nothin' i' their insides, they pinch theirselves in wi' stays. Captain Donnithorne's arm's thicker nor a Frenchmon's body I'll be bound."

Enter DINAH MORRIS L. *with hat on.*

DINAH—"Aunt, I'll be back before dusk."

Exit DINAH R. C. *Closes door after her.*

CRAIG—"Mrs. Poyser, your niece is a well-favored woman." (*sits* L. *of table* L.)

MRS. POYSER—"If Dinah had a bit o' color in her cheeks, an' didn't stick that Methodist cap on her head, folks 'ud think her as pretty as Hetty."

POYSER—"Nay, nay, thee dostna know th' pints of a woman. Th' men 'ud niver run after Dinah as they 'ud after Hetty." (*sits* R. *of table* L.)

Mrs. Poyser—"What care I what th' men 'ud run after? It's well seen what choice th' most of 'em know how to make, by th' poor draggle-tails o' wives you see, like bits o' gauze ribbin, good for nothing when th' color's gone."

Poyser—"Well, well, thee canstna say but what I knowed how to make a choice when I married thee? and thee wast twice as buxom as Dinah, ten years ago."

Mrs. Poyser—"I niver said as a woman had need to be ugly t' make a good missus of a house. There's Chowne's wife, ugly enough to turn th' milk an' save the rennet but she'll niver save anything any other way. She'd take a big cullender to strain her lard wi' an' then wonder as th' scratchin's run through."

Knock at door R. C. *Voice calls:*

"Mrs. Poyser, within?"

MRS. POYSER—(*opens door*) "Come in, Mr. Bede, come in."

Enter ADAM BEDE.

"Poyser, here's Mr. Bede."

POYSER—"Why, to be sure—welcome, Adam, welcome. I'm glad ye're come, sit ye down."

ADAM—"Good evening, Mr. Craig."

CRAIG—"Good evenin', Adam."

ADAM—"I came to see what your spinning wheel wants doing to it."

MRS. POYSER—"I've put it away in the right hand parlor; but let be, till I can fetch an' show it you. Maybe you'd like a drink o' whey, first? I know you're fond o' whey, as most folks is." (*goes to tub* L. C.)

ADAM—"Thank you, Mrs. Poyser, a drink o' whey's allays a treat to me. I'd rather have it than beer, any day."

MRS. POYSER—"Aye, aye. (*reaching a small white cup hanging above the tub and dipping it into the whey tub*) the smell o' bread's sweet t'everybody but the baker. The Misses Irwine allays say, 'O, Mrs. Poyser, I envy you your chickens, an' what a beautiful thing a farm-house is, to be sure.' An' I say, 'Yis, a farm-house is a fine thing, fur them as looks on an' don't know th' liftin' an' th' standin' an' th' worretin' o' th' inside, as belongs to it.' "

Adam—"Why, Mrs. Poyser, you wouldn't like to live any place else but in a farm-house so well as you manage it? There can be nothing to look at pleasanter nor a fine milch cow standing up to its knees in pasture, and the new milk, and the fresh butter ready for market and the calves and the poultry. Here's to your health, and may you allays have strength to look after your own dairy, and set a pattern t' all the farmer's wives in the county."

MRS. POYSER—"Have a little more, Mr. Bede?"

ADAM—"No, thank you. But where's Totty?"

MRS. POYSER—"She's outdoors wi' Hetty—I'd be glad now if you'd go into the garden an' tell Hetty to send Totty in. The child 'ull run in if she's told an' I know Hetty's lettin' her eat too many currants. I'll be much obliged to you, if you'd go an' send her in; an' there's th' York an' Lancaster roses beautiful in th' garden now—you'll like to see 'em."

ADAM—"Anything to oblige you, Mrs. Poyser.

(*going*) I'll go into the garden and send the little lass in."

Mrs. Poyser—"Aye, do; an' tell her, mother says she's wantin' her this minute an' she mustna loiter." (Adam *exits* UPPER R.)

Craig—"Adam Bede's a fine mon. An' he knows a fine sight more o' th' nature o' things than those who think theirselves his betters. He may be workin' fur wages now, but he'll be a master mon some day as sure as I sit i' this chair."

Poyser—"Adam's sure enough, there's no fear but he'll yield well i' th' thrashin'. He's not one o' them as is all straw an' no grain. Master Burge is i' th' right on't, to want him to go partners in his business."

Craig—"An' marry his daughter, if it be true what they say."

Mrs. Poyser—"Indeed! Adam is too smart to look at Mary Burge wi' her yellow face an' hair straight as a hank o' cotton."

Craig—"Maybe, maybe—but the woman as does marry Adam 'ull have a good take, be't Lady-day or Michaelmas."

Mrs. Poyser—"Ah, it's all very well for gells to want a ready-made rich man, but may happen he'll be a ready-made fool; an' it's no use fillin' your pocket full o' money if you've got a hole i' th' corner. I allays said I'd niver marry a man as had got no brains; for where's the use o' a woman's havin' brains o' her own if she's tacked to a geck as everybody's laughin' at? She might as well dress herself fine to sit back-'ard on a donkey."

Craig—"They say as Lisbeth, Adam's mother, objects to his gettin' married; doesna like young women about her."

Poyser—"Eh, it's a poor lookout when th' old folks doesna like th' young 'uns."

Mrs. Poyser—"Aye, it's ill livin' in a hen-roost for them as doesna like fleas. We've all had our turn at bein' young, I reckon, be't good luck or ill."

POYSER—"Come, Rachel, be'nt you forgettin' to offer Mr. Craig some o' your home brewed ale?"

MRS. POYSER—"Aye, I was forgettin'. Molly! Molly! (*enter* MOLLY L.) Go down an' draw some ale." (*enter* TOTTY UPPER R.)

TOTTY—"Did 'ou want me?" (*exit* MOLLY L. C. *going* L.).

MRS. POYSER—"Bless her sweet heart! (*kisses her*) mother allays wants her little pet. If Totty sits down like a good little gell an' keeps quiet (*lifts her up on to the bench*)she may have a sip o' ale from mother's mug." (*exit* MRS. POYSER L.)

CRAIG—"Have you heard any particular news to-day?"

POYSER—"No, not as I remember."

CRAIG—"Ah, they'll keep it close, they'll keep it close, I daresay. But I found it out by chance; an' it's news that may concern Adam (*pause*)—Satchell's got a paralytic stroke. I found it out from the lad they sent to Treddleston for the doctor. He's a good way beyond sixty, you know, an' it's much if he gets over it."

POYSER—"Well, I daresay there'd be more rejoicin' than sorrow i' th' parish at his bein' laid away; for he's been a selfish talebearin' fellow. Though it's th' squire himself as is to blame—hirin' a stupid mon like that to save th' expense o' a proper steward to look arter the estate. When Satchell's laid on the shelf maybe the squire'll put a better mon in his place, but I donna see how it 'ud make any difference to Adam."

CRAIG—"But I see it, I see it. Captain Arthur's comin' o' age now an' it's to be expected he'll ha' a little more say o' things. And I know, an' you know, too, what 'ud be th' captain's wish aboot the woods, if there was a fair opportunity fur makin' a change. He's said in plenty o' people's hearin' that he'd make Adam manager o' th' woods to-morrow if he'd the poo'er."

Enter MRS. POYSER L. *carrying spinning wheel. She places it* R.

MRS. POYSER—"What a time that gell is drawin' th' ale. I think she sets th' jug under an' forgets to turn the tap, as there's nothing you can't believe o' them gells; they'll set th' empty kettle o' the fire an' then come an hour arter to see if the water boils."

POYSER—"She's likely drawin' for the men, too. Thee should'st ha' told her to bring our jug up first."

MRS. POYSER—"Told her? yis, I might spend all the wind i' my body an' take the bellows, too, if I was to tell them gells everything as their own sharpness wonna tell 'em." (*enter* MOLLY L. C. *carrying a large jug, two small mugs and four drinking cans full of beer*) Molly, I niver knew your equals, th' times an' times I've told you. (MOLLY *catches foot in her apron and falls*) There you go! It's what I told you'd come, over an' over again. Th' crockery you've broke sin' you've been in th' house 'ud make a parson swear. God forgi' me for sayin' so; anybody 'ud think you'd got the St. Vitus's dance to see th' things you've throwed down. (*wiping up beer from floor*) It's a pity th' bits wasna stacked up for you to see, though it's neither seein' nor hearin' as 'ull make much odds to you. (MOLLY *begins to cry*) Ah, you'll do no good wi' cryin' an' making more wet to wipe up. (*opening the cupboard door*) An' here I must take the brown an' white jug as hasna been used this three years."

Enter ADAM *carelessly carrying a rose in his hand, and* HETTY *wearing one of* DINAH'S *caps* UPPER R. MRS. POYSER *startled at* HETTY'S *appearance, jug slips from her fingers and breaks.*

MRS. POYSER—"Did iver anybody see the like?. It's them nasty glazed handles—they slip o'er the finger like a snail."

POYSER—"Why, thee'st let thy own whip fly i' thy face."

MRS. POYSER—"It's all very fine to look on an' grin — Hetty, are you mad? whativer do you mean by coming i' that way an' makin' one think as there's a ghost a-walking i' th' house?"

POYSER—"Why, Hetty, lass, are ye turned Methodist? You mun pull your face a deal longer afore you'll do for one. How come ye to put th' cap on?"

HETTY—"Adam said he liked Dinah's looks, an' when I found one o' her caps bleachin' on the grass I put it on. He says folks look better in ugly clothes."

ADAM—"Nay, nay, I only said they seemed to suit Dinah. (aside) But if I said you'd look pretty in 'em I should ha' said nothing but what was true."

POYSER—"Why, Rachel, thee thought'st Hetty war a ghost, didstna? Thee look'dst as scared—"

MRS. POYSER—"It little sinnifies how I looked! It little becomes anybody i' this house to make fun o' my sister's child, they'd be better if they could make theirselves like her i' more ways nor puttin' on her cap." (exit MRS. POYSER with TOTTY into dairy L. C.)

POYSER—"You'd better take the cap off, my lass, it hurts your aunt to see it."

CRAIG—"Well, Poyser, I mun be gettin' on. (rising)

POYSER—"Donna be in a hurry, Craig."

CRAIG—"Thank ye, but I mun go on to see Mcester Massey he wasna at church last Sunday, an' I ha' na seen him for a week past.—Good evenin', Hetty, good evenin', Adam."

ADAM—"Good-evening, Mr. Craig." (exit CRAIG R. C.)

POYSER looks at ADAM and HETTY and exits into dairy L. C. HETTY sits R. of table L. ADAM lays down the rose carefully and examines the spinning wheel R.

ADAM—"Ah, here's a nice bit o' turning wanted.

It's a pretty wheel. I must have it up at the turn-ing shop i' th' village and do the work there. (*looking for a moment at* HETTY) I've been thinking it over in my mind to make it a bit more convenient for doing nice jobs o' cabinet-making at home. I look for me and Seth to get a little business for ourselves i' that way. I've allays done a deal o' such little things in odd hours and they're profitable, for there's more work-manship, nor material in 'em."

HETTY—"Yes, you might be gettin' rich some day. (*pause*) Have you ever been to Eagledale?"

ADAM—"Yes, ten years ago, when I was a lad, I went with father to see about some work there. It's a wonderful sight—rocks and caves, such as you never saw in your life. I never had a right notion o' rocks till I went there."

HETTY—"How long did it take to go?"

ADAM—"The best part o' two days, walking; but it's nothing of a day's journey for anybody as has got a first-rate nag. Captain Arthur goes there a-fishin' sometimes. (*pause*) I wish th' captain'd got th' es-tate in his hands; that 'ud be the right thing for him, for it 'ud give him plenty to do, and he'd do it well, too, for all he's so young; he's got better notions o' things than many a man twice his age. (*pause*) He spoke very handsome to me th' other day about lend-ing me money to set up i' business; and if things come round that way I'd rather be beholden to him nor to any man i' the world. (*leaving the wheel*) If your aunt 'ull send the wheel to Mr. Burge's shop i' the morning, I'll get it done for her by Saturday."

HETTY—"Thank you, Adam, I'll tell her." (*rises*)

ADAM (*taking up the rose*)—"How pretty the roses are now. See, I stole the prettiest, but I didna mean to keep it myself. I think these as are pink and have got a finer sort o' green leaves are prettier than the striped 'uns, don't you?"

HETTY—"Yes, maybe."

ADAM—"It smells sweet, the striped 'uns have no

smell. Stick it in your frock and then you can put it in water after. It 'ud be a pity to let it fade. (HETTY *takes the rose and coquettishly puts it in her hair above the left ear*) Ah, that's like the ladies in the pictures at the Chase; only they've mostly got flowers or feathers, or gold things i' their hair, but somehow I don't like to see 'em; they allays put me i' mind o' the painted women outside the shows at Treddles'on fair. What can a woman have to set her off better than her own hair, when it curls so like yours? If a woman's young and pretty, I think you can see her good looks all the better for her being plain-dressed. It seems to me as a woman's face doesna want flowers. I'm sure yours doesna. It's like a flower itself."

HETTY—"Do you think so?" (*laughs as though not quite understanding.*)

ADAM—"Yes, I like to see you just as you are now; when a man's singing a good tune, he doesna want t' hear bells tinkling and interfering wi' the sound."

HETTY—"O, Adam, what queer things ye do say."

ADAM—"But it's getting near supper time, it'll be pretty near six before I'm at home. And mother may happen to be waiting for me, she's more fidgety nor usual now. Good-night, Hetty."

HETTY—"Good-night, Adam. You'll come again soon?"

ADAM—"Yes, good-night." (*exit* ADAM R. C.)

Enter MR. POYSER *from dairy* L. C.

POYSER—"Has Adam gone?"

HETTY—"Yes."

POYSER—(*pause, gets his tobacco and pipe from shelf above fire-place*) If you can catch Adam for a husband, Hetty, you'll ride i' your own spring cart some day, I'll be your warrant. Ye'll not find many men o' six and twenty as 'll do to put i' the shafts wi' him."

HETTY *moves away pettishly toward* R. C. *and tosses her head.* POYSER *thoughtfully lights his pipe.*

CURTAIN.

ACT SECOND. SCENE FIRST.

IN THE WOOD. LATE AFTERNOON. NEAR THE CHASE.

Stump or log at R. *of stage.*

Enter ARTHUR DONNITHORNE L. *with book under his arm.*

ARTHUR—"I wonder if she'll go home this way? I'd like to see her if she does. Pooh! What an idiot I am. (*sits* R.) What does it concern me whether Hetty Sorrel walks this way or not? (*pause*) But why shouldn't I treat the little thing kindly?—She's a beauty and no mistake. Perhaps, I would better take no more notice of her; it may put notions into her head, as Mrs. Irwine thinks. By Jove! there she comes now. Tripping along in her bright colors she looks like a bird among the boughs."

Enter HETTY SORREL R. *with a basket on her arm. Courtesies to* ARTHUR.

ARTHUR—"You are quite right to choose this way of going and coming from the Chase. It is so much prettier as well as shorter than by either of the lodges."

HETTY—"Yes, sir."

ARTHUR—"Did you learn anything from Mrs. Pomfret this afternoon?"

HETTY—"Yes, sir: she says as I'm doing fine, and in a few more lessons I'll be able to mend lace as well as she can."

ARTHUR—"Really? You must be an apt pupil. Though for that matter no one could look at those bright eyes of yours and think to the contrary."

HETTY—"She's teaching me cutting out, too."

ARTHUR—"What, are you going to be a lady's maid?"

HETTY—"I should like to be one."

ARTHUR—"I suppose your aunt will be on the look-out and expecting you home about this time, won't she?"

HETTY—"Yes, sir."

ARTHUR—"Ah, then I must not keep you now, else I should like to show you The Hermitage. Did you ever see it?"

HETTY—"No, sir."

ARTHUR—"It's my den, where I go when I want to get away from everybody, to read and write and study. This is the walk where we would turn up to it. But we must not go now. Some other time I'll show it to you if you'd like to see it?"

HETTY—"Yes, please, sir."

ARTHUR—"Do you always come back this way in the evening, or are you afraid to take so lonely a road?"

HETTY—"Oh, no, sir, it's never late; I allays set out by eight o'clock and it's so light now in the evening. My aunt 'ud be very cross wi' me if I didn't get home before nine."

ARTHUR—"Perhaps, Craig, the gardener, comes to take care of you?"

HETTY—"I'm sure he doesna; I'm sure he never did; I wouldn't let him. I don't like him." (*tears of vexation come to her eyes.*)

ARTHUR—"Why, Hetty, what makes you cry? I didn't mean to vex you. I wouldn't vex you for the world, you little blossom—(*playfully pinches her arm*) come, don't cry. Look at me, else I'll think you won't forgive me. (HETTY *drops her basket*) Has something frightened you, Hetty? Have you seen anything in the wood? Don't be frightened,—I'll take care of you, now. Come, be cheerful again. Smile at me and tell me what is the matter. Come, tell me."

HETTY (*softly*)—"I thought you wouldn't come."

ARTHUR—"You little frightened bird! (*puts his arm around her and kisses her.*) Little tearful rose! Silly pet! You won't cry again now I'm with you, will you?"

HETTY—"No."

ARTHUR—"I wish I could always hold you in my arms tight, just like this. Would you like me to, Hetty?"

HETTY (*softly*)—"Yes."

ARTHUR—"You would, eh? (*kisses her again*) You sweet wild rose! You're coming to my birthday feast on the 30th, aren't you?"

HETTY—"Yes."

ARTHUR—"And you'll give me the dances I've asked for?"

HETTY—"Yes."

ARTHUR—"If you don't, I shall be the most miserable man in the world. (*starts*) What's that? There's some one coming! You go back towards the Chase as if you'd forgotten something. I'll go this way. Till to-morrow." (*exits hastily* L.)

Enter DINAH MORRIS *and* SETH BEDE R. HETTY *starts back toward the Chase* R.

DINAH—"Why, Hetty, where is thee going?"

HETTY—"Back to the Chase."

DINAH—"Hurry, child, and I will wait for thee here. It is growing late." (*exit* HETTY R.) "Hetty must have forgotten something. She's been at the Chase this afternoon. Mrs. Pomfret, the lady's-maid, has a kind heart and is teaching the child to make lace." (*sits* R. SETH *x's to* L.)

SETH—"You've quite made up your mind to go back to Snowfield, Dinah?"

DINAH—"Yea, I'm called there. It was borne in upon my mind on Sunday as Sister Allen, who's in a decline, is in need of me."

SETH—"Hast heard from her, Dinah?"

DINAH—"By a vision, yea, I saw her as plain as we see that bit of white cloud yonder. She was lifting up her poor, thin hand and beckoning to me. And this morning when I opened the Bible for direction the first words my eyes fell on were, 'And after he had seen the vision, immediately we endeavored to go into Macedonia.' If it wasn't for that clear showing of the Lord's will I should be loath to go, for my heart yearns over my aunt and her little ones and Hetty Sorrel. I've been much drawn out in prayer for Hetty of late, and I look on it as a token that there may be mercy in store for her."

SETH—"God grant it. For I doubt Adam is so set on her he'll never turn to anybody else; and if he was to marry her, I canna think as she'd make him happy. It's a deep mystery—the way a man's heart turns to one woman out of all the rest he's seen i' the world, and makes it easier for him to work seven year for her, like Jacob did for Rachel, sooner than have any other woman for the asking. After what you told me o' your mind last Saturday, mayhappen you'll think me over bold to speak to you about it again, but I've been thinking it over by night and by day, and it seems to me there's more texts for your marryin' than ever you could find against it. For St. Paul says as plain as can be, 'I will that the younger women marry,' (*quickly*) an' two are better than one, Dinah, an' that holds good wi' marriage as well as wi' other things. We should be o' one heart and o' one mind, an' I'd never be the husband to make a claim on you as 'ud interfere wi' your work. I'd make a shift and fend indoor and out, to give you more liberty—more than you have now, and I'm strong enough to work for us both."

DINAH— (*pause*) "Seth Bede, I thank thee for thy love toward me, and if I could think of any man as more than a Chistian brother, it would be you. When I first saw as your love was given to me, I thought it might be a leading of Providence for me to change my way of life, and that we should be fellow helpers, but whenever I tried to fix my heart on our living together, other thoughts always came in—thoughts of the sick and dying. And so I see that I have been called to minister to others, and not to have joys and sorrows of my own."

SETH—"Dinah, perhaps, I oughtn't to feel for any creature as I feel for you, for I can't help saying of you what the hymn says, 'She is my soul's bright morning star.' That may be wrong, and I'm to be taught better. (*pause*) You wouldn't be displeased wi' me if things turned out so as I could leave this country an' go to live at Snowfield, an' be near you?"

DINAH—"No, but I counsel you not to leave your own country and kindred lightly. We mustn't be in a hurry to choose our own lot."

SETH—"There is no knowin' but what you may see things different after awhile. There may be a new leading?"

DINAH—"Let us leave that, Seth. It is good to live only a moment at a time. It isn't for you and me to lay plans; we've nothing to do but to obey and to trust. Good-bye."

SETH—"Good-bye. (*going* L.) You'd let me write you a letter, Dinah, if there was anything I wanted to tell you?"

DINAH—"Yea, and you'll be continually in my prayers. Farewell."

SETH—"Farewell, Dinah." (*exit* SETH L.)

Enter HETTY R.

DINAH—"I'm glad you've come, Hetty, it's time we were at the Hall Farm. (DINAH *takes* HETTY's *hand and draws it under her own arm*) Dear child, how happy you look. I shall think of you often when I'm at Snowfield, and see your face before me as it is now. It's a strange thing—sometimes when I'm alone in my room or walking over the hills, the people

I've known are brought before me, and I hear their voices and see their looks. And I am sure that you will come before me, for I feel strongly drawn to you. If you are ever in need of a friend, Hetty, come to Dinah Morris at Snowfield."

HETTY—"Why should you think of trouble comin' to me."

DINAH—"Because, dear, trouble comes to us all in this life, and then we need friends."

HETTY—"Oh, yes—Have you been over to the Bede's again to-day?"

DINAH—"Yea. It has been very precious to me seeing two such good sons as Adam and Seth Bede. Mrs. Bede has been telling me what Adam has done for these many years to help his father and his brother. It's wonderful what a spirit of wisdom he has, and how he's ready to use it in behalf of them that are feeble. And I'm sure he has a loving spirit, too. Don't you think so, Hetty?"

HETTY—"Yes I suppose he has."

DINAH—"But come, Hetty, dear, we must not give aunt cause for worriment."

Exit DINAH *and* HETTY L.

End of Scene First, Act Second.

ACT SECOND. SCENE SECOND.

THE BIRTHDAY FEAST.   AFTERNOON.

THE CHASE LAWN.

BEFORE AND AT RISE OF CURTAIN BELLS HEARD RINGING. BUNTING AND FLAGS HUNG ABOUT.

VILLAGERS AND TENANTS MOVING ABOUT THE STAGE.

THE CHASE LAWN.

RAISED DAIS ERECTED R. ON WHICH RESTS ELABORATE GOLD CHAIR. TABLE L. SLIGHTLY RAISED FROM FLOOR. TABLE DOWN R. TABLE C. AT BACK. ALL THE TABLES DECORATED AND BRIGHT WITH CUT GLASS AND SILVER AND FLOWERS. SMALL TABLE NEAR DAIS ON WHICH ARE PILED NEATLY WRAPPED PACKAGES.

Enter MR. *and* MRS. POYSER, *old* MARTIN POYSER, TOTTY *and* HETTY L.

MRS. POYSER—"Why, the Chase is like a fair. I shouldna ha' thought there was so many people i' th' two parishes. Massey on us, how hot it is! Come here, Totty, keep i' the shade else your little face 'ull be burned to a scratchin'. They might ha' cooked the dinner i' that open space an' saved the fires. Father, there's Mr. Taft, dost remember him?"

OLD POYSER—"Aye, aye, I remember Jacob Taft walkin' fifty mile arter the Scotch reybels, when they turned back from Stoniton. (*goes toward* TAFT, *shouts in his ear*) Well, Meester Taft, you're hearty yit. You can enjoy yoursen to-day, for all your ninety an' better."

TAFT—"Your sarvent, Meester Poyser, your sarvent." (*they move aside*)

Enter ADAM, SETH *and* LISBETH BEDE L.

MILLS (*to* ADAM)—"Beg pardon, sir, Captain Donnithorne's compliments and it is his particular wish that you dine with the large tenants to-day." (MILLS *moves aside.*)

ADAM (*to* SETH)—"Seth, lad, the captain has sent word as I'm to sit with the large tenants, he wishes it particular, the butler says; I suppose it 'ud be behavin' ill for me not to do it. I don't like sitting above thee and mother, though, as if I was better than my own flesh and blood. Thee't not take it unkind, I hope?"

SETH—"Nay, nay, Adam, thy honor's our honor; and if thee gets respect thee'st won it by thy own deserts. It's because o' thy being appointed over the woods, thee't above a common workman now."

ADAM—"Aye, but nobody knows a word about it yet. People 'ull be wondering to see me there, and they'll like enough be guessin' the reason, and askin' questions."

SETH—"Well, thee canst say, thee wast ordered to come wi'out being told the reason. That's the truth. Mother 'ull be fine and joyful about it, I'll go and tell her." (*goes to* LISBETH)

MILLS (C.)—"Ladies and gentlemen."

From the crowd—"Hear! hear!"

MILLS—"Captain Donnithorne's best wishes and will you please take your places at table." (*crowd begin sitting at tables, except at table slightly raised from the floor* L. MRS. POYSER, HETTY *and* TOTTY, LISBETH BEDE *and* SETH BEDE *sit at table* R.)

ADAM (*to* CRAIG)—"Well, Mr. Craig, I'm going to sit with you to-day; the captain's sent me orders."

CRAIG—"Ah, then there's somethin' i' th' wind, there's somethin' i' th' wind. Ha' you heard anything about what the old squire means to do?"

ADAM—"I'll tell you what I know if you'll promise to keep a still tongue in your head?"

CRAIG—"Trust ta me, my boy, trust ta me. I've got na wife to worm it out o' me an' thin run out an' cackle it i' iverybody's hearin'. If you trust a mon, let him be a bachelor—let him be a bachelor."

ADAM—"Well, then, it was settled yesterday that I'm to take the management o' th' woods. But if anybody asks questions just you take no notice, an' turn th' talk to something else."

CRAIG—"I know what to do, niver fear. The news

'ull be good sauce to my dinner, though. Mark what I tell you, ye'll get on." (*they go towards table* L. *where the crowd are unable to decide about places.*)

CASSON—"It stands to sense, as old Mr. Poyser, as the old mon should sit at the top o' th' table."

OLD POYSER—"Nay, nay, I'm gi'en up to my son; I'm no tenant now; let my son take my place. The ould folks ha' had their turn; they mun make way for the young 'uns."

CRAIG—"I should ha' thought the biggest tenant had the best right more nor the eldest. There's Meester Holdsworth has more land nor anybody else on th' estate."

POYSER—"Well, suppose we say the mon wi' the foulest land shall sit at top; when whoiver gets th' honor, there'll be no envyin' on him."

CRAIG—"Eh, here's Meester Massey, the schoolmaster ought to be able to tell what's right. Who's to sit at the top of the table, Meester Massey?"

MASSEY—"Why, the broadest man; and then he won't take up other folks' room; and the next broadest must sit at bottom." (*laughter and confusion of taking places.*)

CRAIG—"Well, Meester Massey, who air the broadest men?"

MASSEY—"Martin Poyser, the younger, to be sure. He must sit at head o' table and Mr. Casson at the bottom."

CRAIG—"Nay, Adam Bede must sit at bottom. He's broader nor Meester Casson."

MASSEY—"True, Adam Bede must sit at bottom."

(*All sit,* MARTIN POYSER *at head,* ADAM BEDE *at bottom of table.* CASSON *provoked that he is supplanted by* ADAM)

CASSON—"Well, Mr. Bede, you're one o' them as mounts hup'ards apace. You've niver dined wi' th' large tenants afore as I remember?"

ADAM—"No, Mr. Casson, I've never dined here before—but I come by Captain Donnithorne's wish, and
I hope it's not disagreeable to anybody here?"

Several voices—"Nay, nay, we're glad ye're come.
Who's got anything to say agin' it?"

MASSEY—"You'll sing us 'Over the hills and far
away,' after dinner, won't you Mr. Casson? That's a
song I'm uncommonly fond of."

CRAIG—"Peeh! It's not to be named beside o' the
Scotch tunes. I've niver cared much about singin'
myself, but a second cousin of mine, a drover, was a
rare hand at rememberin' th' Scotch tunes. He'd got
nothin' else to think on."

CASSON—"The Scotch tunes! I've heard enough o'
them Scotch tunes to last me while I live. They're fit
fur nothin' but to frighten th' birds with—that's to say,
the English birds, fur the Scotch birds may sing Scotch,
fur what I know." (*laughter*)

CRAIG—"Yes, there's folks as find a pleasure in
undervalying what they know little about."

HETTY (*at the other table*)—"O, aunt, I wish you'd
speak to Totty, she keeps puttin' her legs up so, and
messin' my frock."

MRS. POYSER—"What's the matter with the child?
She can niver please you. Let her come up by th' side
o 'me, I can put up wi' her." (TOTTY *changes her place
to her mother*)

BENEFIT CLUB BAND *heard playing* HAIL TO THE
CHIEF, R.

MRS. POYSER—"The captain's comin'! I hope Poyser won't get tripped up wi' his speech o' welcome and
stop i' th' middle, like a balky horse."

Enter BENEFIT CLUB BAND R. *followed by* ARTHUR
DONNITHORNE *and* REV. ADOLPHUS IRWINE. ARTHUR
*dressed in full regimentals. Clapping of hands, waving
of handkerchiefs, and general demonstrations of good
feeling for* ARTHUR.

ARTHUR (C.)—"My grandfather and I hope all our friends here are enjoying their dinner and find my birthday ale good. Mr. Irwine and I are come to taste it with you."

MR. POYSER *rises deliberately, with his hands in his pockets.*

POYSER—"Captain, my neighbors ha' put it upo' me to speak for 'em to-day, for where folks think pretty much alike, one spokesman's as good as a score. And though we've mayhappen got contrairy ways o' thinkin' about a many things—this I'll say, as we're all o' one mind about our young squire. We've pretty nigh all on us known you when you war a little 'un an' we've niver known anything on you but what was good an' honorable. You speak fair an' y' act fair, an' we're joyful when we look forrard to your bein' our landlord, for we believe you mean to do right by iverybody, an' 'ull make no man's bread bitter to him if you can help it. That's what I mean, an' that's what we all mean; an' when a man's said what he means he'd better stop, fur th' ale 'ull be none the better fur stannin'. And I'll not say how we like the ale yit, for we warna goin' to taste it till we'd drunk your health in it; but the dinner is good, an' if there's anybody isna enjoyin' it, it must be the fault o' his own inside. An' as fur the rector's company, it's well known as that's welcome t' all the parish wheriver he may be; and I hope as he'll live to see us old folks, an' our children grown to men and women, an' your honor a man o' family. I've no more to say as concerns the present time, an' so we'll drink our young squire's health— three times three!" (*Shouting, rapping, a jingling of glasses, etc.*)

ARTHUR—"I thank you all, my good friends and neighbors, for the good opinion of me and the kind feelings which Mr. Poyser has been expressing on your behalf and on his own. It will always be my heartiest wish to deserve them. If I live, we may expect that I shall one day be your landlord. It hardly becomes a man of my age to talk about farming to you, who are most of you so much older, and men of experience; still I have interested myself in such matters and learned as much about them as my opportunities have allowed; and when the course of events shall place the estate in my hands it will be my first desire to afford my tenants all the encouragement a landlord can give them. It will be my wish to be looked on by all my tenants as their best friend, and nothing would make me so happy as to be able to respect every man on the estate, and in return, to be respected by him. I meet your good hopes concerning me by telling you that my own hopes correspond to them—that what you expect from me I desire to fulfill; and I am quite of Mr. Poyser's opinion that when a man has said what he means he would better stop. But the pleasure I feel in having my own health drunk by you would not be perfect if we did not drink the health of my grandfather, who has filled the place of both father and mother to me. I will say no more until you have joined me in drinking his health." (*all drink.*)

MRS. POYSER—"The captain had better not ha' stirred a kettle o' sour broth. I'll not drink to the old man's health."

ARTHUR—"I thank you, both for my grandfather and for myself; and now there is one thing more I wish to tell you, that you may share my happiness about it. I think there can be no man here who has not a respect, and some of you, I am sure, have a very high regard for my friend, Adam Bede. It is well known to everyone in this neighborhood, that there is no man whose word can be more depended upon than his; that whatever he undertakes to do, he does well and is as careful for the interests of those who employ him as for his own. I am proud to say that I was very fond of Adam when I was a little boy, and I have never lost my old feeling for him—I think that shows

that I know a good fellow when I see him. (*applause*)
It has been my wish that he should have the management of the valuable wood-land on the estate, both
because I think so highly of his character, and because
he has the knowledge and the skill which fit him for
the place. I am happy to tell you that it is my grandfather's wish, too, and it is now settled that Adam
shall manage the woods—and by and by, I hope you
will join me in drinking his health. But there is a
still older friend of mine than Adam Bede present, Mr.
Irvine. I'm sure you will agree with me that we must
drink no other person's health until we have drunk
his. I know you all have reason to love him, but no
one of his parishioners has so much reason as I.
Come, charge your glasses and let us drink to our
excellent rector—three times three!" (*the toast is
drunk with enthusiasm.* ARTHUR *steps up on the dais,
looks about, then sits.*)

REV. IRWINE—"This is not the first time by a great
many that I have had to thank my parishioners for
giving me tokens of their good will, but neighborly
kindness is among those things that are the more
precious the older they get. Indeed, our pleasant
meeting to-day is a proof that when what is good
comes of age and is likely to live, there is reason for
rejoicing, and the relation between us as clergyman
and parishioners came of age two years ago, for it is
three and twenty years since I first came among you,
and I see some tall, fine looking young men here, as
well as some blooming young women, that were far
from looking as pleasantly at me when I christened
them, (*laughter*) as I am happy to see them looking
now. But you will not wonder when I say, that among
all those young men, the one in whom I have the
strongest interest, is my friend, Captain Arthur Donnithorne, for whom you have just expressed your
regard. I had the pleasure of being his tutor for several years and have naturally had opportunities of
knowing him intimately which cannot have occurred

to anyone else who is present; and I have some pride as well as pleasure in assuring you that I share your high hopes concerning him, and your confidence in his possession of those qualities which will make him an excellent landlord when the time shall come for him to take that important position among you. We feel alike on most matters on which a man who is getting toward fifty, can feel in common with a young man of one and twenty, and he has just been expressing a feeling which I share very heartily, and I would not willingly omit the opportunity of saying so. That feeling is his value and respect for Adam Bede. People in a high station are of course more thought of and talked about and have their virtues more praised than those whose lives are passed in humble, everyday work; but every sensible man knows how necessary that humble, everyday work is, and how important to us that it should be well done. When a man whose duty lies in that sort of work shows a character which would make him an example in any station, his merit should be acknowledged. He is one of those to whom honor is due, and his friends should delight to honor him. I know Adam Bede well. I know what he is as a workman, and what he has been as a son and a brother, and I am saying the simplest truth when I say that I respect him as much as I respect any man living. But I am not speaking to you about a stranger, some of you are his intimate friends, and I believe there is not one here who does not know enough of him to join heartily in drinking his health."

ARTHUR (*jumps up filling his glass*)—"A bumper to Adam Bede, and may he live to have sons as faithful and as clever as himself!" (*all drink*)

ADAM—"I'm quite taken by surprise. I didn't expect anything o' this sort, for it's a good deal more than my wages. But I've the more reason to be grateful to you, captain, and to you, Mr. Irwine, and to all my friends here, who've drunk my health and wished me well. It 'ud be nonsense for me to be saying, I don't at all deserve th' opinion you have o' me; that 'ud be poor thanks to you, to say that you've known me all these years and yet haven't sense enough to find out a great deal of truth about me. You think if I undertake to do a bit o' work, I'll do it well, be my pay big or little—and that's true. I'd be ashamed to stand before you here, if it wasna true. But it seems to me that's a man's plain duty, and nothing to be conceited about; for let us do what we will, it's only making use o' the sperrit and the powers as ha' been given to us. And so, this kindness o' yours I'm sure is no debt you owe me, but a free gift, and as such I accept it, and am thankful. And as to this new employment, I've taken in hand, I'll only say that I took it at Captain Donnithorne's desire, and that I'll try to fulfill his expectations. I'd wish for no better lot than to work under him, and to know while I was getting my own bread I was taking care of his int'rests. For I believe he's one o' those gentlemen as wishes to do the right thing, and to leave the world a bit better than he found it, which it's my belief every man may do whether he's gentle or simple. There's no occasion for me to say any more about what I feel toward him—I hope to show it through the rest o' my life in my actions."

(ADAM *sits amid a clapping of hands.* ARTHUR *goes to him and shakes his hand warmly, then exits* R. *There is a general movement of rising from tables. Butlers move tables from the stage*)

REV. IRWINE (*to* MRS. POYSER)—"How do you do, Mrs. Poyser? Weren't you pleased to hear your husband make such a good speech to-day?"

MRS. POYSER—"O, sir, the men are mostly so tonguetied you're forced partly to guess what they mean, as you do wi' the dumb creatures."

REV. IRWINE—"What? You think you could have made it better for him? (*laughing*)

MRS. POYSER—"Well, sir, when I want to say any-

thing, I can mostly find words to say it in. Not as I'm
a finding faut wi' my husband, for, if he's a man o' few
words, what he says he'll stan' to."

Rev. Irwine (*looking around*)—"I'm sure I never
saw a prettier party than this."

Mrs. Poyser—"If I'm not too inquisitive, where is
Mrs. Irwine and the Misses Irwine?"

Rev. Irwine—"They will be here presently. Captain Donnithorne has gone to fetch them. They would
have come before, but they were afraid of the noise
of the toasts. Ah, here they are now."

Enter Arthur Donnithorne *leading* Mrs. Irwine,
*dressed in damask satin, jewels and black lace, followed
by the* Misses Irwine. Mrs. Irwine *sits on the
dais* R.

Mrs. Irwine (*looking about*)—"Upon my word it's
a pretty sight, and it's the last fête-day I'm likely to
see, unless you make haste and get married, Arthur.
But take care you get a charming bride; else I would
rather die without seeing her."

Arthur—"You are so terribly fastidious, godmother, I'm afraid I shall never satisfy you with my
choice."

Mrs. Irwine—"But I won't forgive you if she's not
handsome, and she must not be silly; that will never
do, because you'll want managing, and a silly woman
could never manage you."

Rev. Irwine—"What's this—something you've ar-
ranged, Arthur? Here's Joshua Rann with his fiddle
and Wiry Ben with a nosegay in his buttonhole."

Arthur—"Excuse me for a moment, godmother."
(*leaves her and goes to* C. *of stage.*) Now, friends,
we're going to have the pleasure of seeing Wiry Ben
dance the hornpipe, then we're going to listen to some
singing by Mr. Casson, and then—but I mustn't tell you
all we're going to do, must I? else there'll be no sur-
prises. But before we begin let me say this, I'm never

going to be twenty-one again, (*laughter*) and I want you all to have so good a time that you'll never forget the day I came of age. Now, Wiry Ben."

(ARTHUR *goes back to the side of* MRS. IRWINE. WIRY BEN, *to the playing of the fiddle by* JOSHUA RANN, *dances the hornpipe. Applause when* BEN *finishes.*)

POYSER (*to* MRS. POYSER)—"What dost think o' that? He goes as pat to the music as if he was made o' clock work. I used to be a pretty good 'un at dancin' myself, but I could niver ha' hit it just to the hair like that."

MRS. POYSER—"It's little matter what his legs are, he's empty enough i' the upper story, or he'd niver come jiggin' and stampin' like a mad grasshopper. The gentry are fit to die wi' laughin'."

POYSER—"Well, well, so much the better if it amuses 'em."

(ARTHUR *moves about and arranges for the next number on the programme.*)

MRS. IRWINE—"Who is that tall young man, Dauphin, with the mild face? There standing without his hat and taking such care of that old woman by the side of him—his mother, of course. I like to see that."

REV. IRWINE—"Why, don't you know him, mother? That is Seth Bede, Adam's brother—a Methodist, but a very good fellow."

MRS. IRWINE—"He looks rather downhearted."

REV. IRWINE—"Yes, I thought it was because of his father's recent death, but Joshua Rann tells me he wants to marry that sweet little Methodist preacher, Dinah Morris, staying at Poyser's. Perhaps, she has refused him."

MRS. IRWINE—"Ah, I remember hearing Mr. Rann tell about her; but there's no end of gossip that man can repeat. We must not listen with credence to all he says."

(With awkward movement MR. CASSON *comes forward* C., *bows first to* MRS. IRWINE,*then to the crowd. Sings an English ballad, is given an encore.* CASSON *gives a look of triumph at* CRAIG *as he finally takes his place among the crowd.)*

CRAIG—"It's a true sayin', there's no accountin' fur tastes. A crowd that 'ud applaud such bawlin 'ud niver care t' hear th' sweet Scotch tunes, as my second cousin can sing."

ARTHUR (C.)—"Now, friends, Signor Partie, of London, will entertain us. He has brought his little boy and girl with him—they are very intelligent children, so you must listen carefully to what they say."

(A chair is placed in the C. of stage and a ventriloquist entertains the crowd. When he has finished and retired, dialogue continues.)

REV. IRWINE—"There are the Poysers, mother, not far off on the right hand. Mrs. Poyser is looking at you. Do take notice of her."

MRS. IRWINE—"To be sure I will. (*bows graciously to* MRS. POYSER) A woman who sends me such excellent cream cheese is not to be neglected. Bless me, what a cunning little child she is holding on her knee. But who is that pretty girl with dark eyes?"

REV. IRWINE—"That is Hetty Sorrel, Martin Poyser's niece. A very likely young person and well looking, too. She has lived with the Poysers six or seven years. You must have seen her, mother."

MRS. IRWINE—"No, I've not seen her, son; at least not as she is now. (ARTHUR *comes up to* MRS. IRWINE.) Godson. I quite agree with you, Hetty Sorrel is a Hebe. What a pity such beauty should be thrown away among the farmers, when it's wanted so terribly among the good families without fortune. Mind, that doesn't apply to you, godson. (ARTHUR *laughingly moves away*) I daresay now, the girl will marry a man who would have thought her just as pretty if she had round eyes and red hair."

REV. IRWINE—"No, mother, I can't agree with you there. The commonest man is conscious of the difference between a lovely, delicate woman and a coarse one."

MRS. IRWINE—"Bless me! Dauphin, what does an old bachelor like you know about it?"

REV. IRWINE—"That is one of the matters in which old bachelors are wiser than married men, because they have time for more general contemplation."

MRS. IRWINE—"O, Dauphin, Dauphin!"

ARTHUR (C.)—"Next on the programme, friends, will be the games."

Women attempt to walk as many yards as possible on one leg—Donkey races etc., etc. Band stops playing.

ARTHUR—"The winners will now receive their prizes from Mrs. Irwine."

The MISSES IRWINE hand packages from small table to their mother. CHAD'S BESS is the first to come forward.

REV. IRWINE—"This is Bessy Cranage, mother, Chad Cranage's daughter. You remember Chad Cranage, the blacksmith?"

MRS. IRWINE—"Yes, to be sure. Well, Bessy, here is your prize—excellent warm things for winter. I'm sure you've had hard work to win them this warm day." (*girl courtesies and walks away dejectedly*)

ARTHUR—"You didn't think the winner was to be so young, I suppose, godmother. Couldn't we find something else for this girl and give that gown to one of the older women? I think she's disappointed."

Mrs. Irwine—"It is best as it is, godson; for a love of finery must not be encouraged in young women of that class. Nothing has been provided but what is useful and substantial."

(*While prizes are being given out the following dialogue takes place down* L.)

Adam (*to* Lisbeth)—"After the prizes are given out they're going to have dancin'—Captain Donnithorne wants me to join in."

Lisbeth—"Eh! it's fine talkin' o' dancin', and thy fayther not long in's grave. I wish I war there too, i'stid o' bein' left to take up merrier folks' room above ground."

Adam—"Nay, don't look at i' that way, mother— I don't mean to dance, I shall only look on. And since the captain wishes me to be here. it 'ud look as if I thought I knew better than him, to say as I'd rather not stay. And thee know'st how he's behaved to me to-day."

Lisbeth—"Eh! Thee't do as thee lik'st for thy old mother's got no right t' hinder thee. She's naught but the old husks, and thee'st slipped away from her like the ripe nut."

Adam—"Well, mother, I'll go to tell the captain as it hurts thy feelings for me to stay and I'd rather go home upon that account; he won't take it ill then, I dare say, and I'm willing."

Lisbeth—"Nay, nay, I wonna ha' thee do that— the young squire 'ull be angered. Go and do what thee't ordered to do, an' me an' Seth 'ull go home. I know it's a great honor for thee to be so looked on— an' who's prouder on it nor thy mother?"

Adam—"Well, good-bye then, mother—good-bye lad—remember to feed Gyp when you get home." (*exit* Lisbeth *and* Seth Bede l.)

Poyser (*comes up to* Adam *with* Totty *on his shoulder,* Hetty *beside him*)—"Well, Adam, I'm glad

to get sight on y' again. You're going to ha' a bit o'
fun now I hope. And here's Hetty has promised no
end o' partners, an' I've just been askin' her if she'd
agree'd to dance wi' you, an' she says no."

ADAM—"Well, I didn't think o' dancin' to-day."

POYSER—"Nonsense! Why, iverybody's goin' to
dance, except Mrs. Irwine. The young squire has
picked out Hetty to be his first partner; she niver had
such a partner afore. It'll serve you to talk on, Hetty,
when you are an old woman—how you danced wi'
th' young squire the day he come o' age. But you'll
dance wi' Adam after that, won't you, Hetty?"

HETTY—"I've got no partner for the fourth dance.
I'll dance that wi' you if you like." (MRS. POYSER
joins the group.)

POYSER—"You canna for shame stand still, Adam,
an' you a fine young fellow an' can dance as well as
anybody."

MRS. POYSER—"Nay, nay, it 'ud be unbecomin'. I
know the dancin's nonsense; but if you stick at iverything because it's nonsense, you wonna go far i' this
life."

ADAM—"Then, if Hetty 'ull dance wi' me, I'll dance
the fourth dance."

POYSER—"Ah! but you mun dance the first dance,
Adam, else it 'ull look partic'lar. There's plenty o'
nice partners to pick an' choose from, an' it's hard
for the gells when the men stan' by and don't ask 'em.
Hetty, take the little 'un while I go an' hunt a partner." (HETTY *takes* TOTTY *in her arms.* MRS. POY-
SER *moves toward* c. *and intercepts* ARTHUR *as he
passes.*)

MRS. POYSER—"I've desired Hetty to remember as
she's got to dance wi' you, first, sir, for she's so
thoughtless she'd be like enough to go an' engage herself for ivery dance."

ARTHUR—"Thank you, Mrs. Poyser." (*a partner
claims* MRS. POYSER, *who moves away*)

ADAM (*to* HETTY)—"Let me hold the child for you,

Hetty. Children are so heavy when they're asleep."
(*in changing* TOTTY *from* HETTY *to* ADAM, *she wakes
up and peevishly strikes at* ADAM, *in doing so she
catches her hand in a chain about* HETTY'S *neck. A
locket leaps out from* HETTY'S *frock, chain breaks and
locket falls on the floor*)

HETTY—"My locket! my locket! never mind the
beads."

ADAM (*picks up locket*)—"It's all right, it isn't
hurt."

HETTY (*suddenly regaining her composure*)—"Oh,
it doesn't matter. I don't mind about it."

ADAM—"No matter? You seemed very frightened
about it a second ago."

HETTY—"See, (*taking locket*) they're taking their
places to dance."

(ARTHUR *comes toward* HETTY.)

ARTHUR—"Are you ready, Miss Hetty? You know
the first dance has been promised to me and I won't
give it up to any one. (*as they move away* ARTHUR
says aside to her)   My sweet, you look more lovely
than ever to-day. I shall be in the wood the day after
to-morrow at seven; come as early as you can."

(ARTHUR *makes a motion for the music to begin.
Band strikes up and they dance a country dance with
spirit.* ADAM *stands aside meditatively holding*
TOTTY.)

CURTAIN.

ACT THIRD. SCENE FIRST.

—————

IN THE GROVE. (TWO DAYS LATER.) THE HERMITAGE.

EARLY EVENING IN SUMMER.

RUSTIC HOUSE R. (END OF HOUSE TO THE AUDIENCE) DOOR L. IN CENTRE OF HOUSE. RUSTIC TABLE L. RUSTIC CHAIR R. OF TABLE. STUMP DOWN L.

Door of the Hermitage opens and ARTHUR *and* HETTY *come out hand in hand—*ARTHUR *is dressed in evening clothes.*

ARTHUR—"You must hurry home, now, my little pet. It is growing late. Good-night. (*folds her to his breast and kisses her passionately*)

(*Enter* ADAM BEDE R. *with stick over his shoulder on which is hung a basket of tools.* ARTHUR *and* HETTY *quickly separate,* HETTY *exits hastily* L. ADAM *stands motionless looking at* ARTHUR.)

ARTHUR (*pause*)—"Well, Adam, you're on your way home from work, I presume? I overtook pretty Hetty Sorrel as I was coming to my den, the Hermitage, here. So, I took care of her and asked a kiss for my pains. But I must get back now, (*going* R.) for this road is confoundedly damp. Good-night, Adam, I shall see you to-morrow to say good-bye, you know." (*starts to leave*)

ADAM—"Stop a bit, sir! I've got a word to say to you."

ARTHUR—"What do you mean, Adam?"

ADAM—"I mean, sir, I mean, sir, that you don't deceive me by your light words. By your actions, this is not the first time you've met Hetty Sorrel in this grove, and this is not the first time you've kissed her."

ARTHUR—"Well, sir, what then?"

ADAM—"Why, then, instead of acting like th' upright, honorable man we've all believed you to be, you've been acting the part of a selfish, light-minded scoundrel. You know as well as I do, what it's to lead to, when a gentleman kisses and makes love to a young woman like Hetty, and gives her presents as she's frightened for other folks to see. And though it cuts me to th' heart to say so, I say it again, you're acting the part of a selfish, light-minded scoundrel!"

ARTHUR—"Let me tell you, Adam, you're not only devilish impertinent, but you're talking nonsense. Every pretty girl isn't such a fool as to suppose that when a gentleman admires her beauty and pays her a little attention, he must mean something particular. Every man likes to flirt with a pretty girl and every pretty girl likes to be flirted with. The wider social distance there is between them the less harm there is, for then she's not likely to deceive herself."

ADAM—"I don't know what you mean by flirting, but if you mean behaving to a woman as if you loved her, and yet not loving her all the while, I say that's no' th' action of an honest man, and what isn't honest comes t' harm. I'm not a fool, and you're not a fool, and you know better than what you're saying. You know it couldn't be made public as you've behaved to Hetty, without her losing her character and bringing shame and trouble on her and on her relatives. What if you meant nothing by your kissing and your presents; other folks won't believe as you've meant nothing; and don't tell me about her not deceiving herself. I tell you as you've so filled her mind with the thought of you, that she'll never love another man as 'ud make her a good husband."

ARTHUR—"Well, Adam, perhaps, I have gone a little too far in taking notice of the pretty thing and stealing a kiss now and then. I'm sure I wouldn't bring any trouble or annoyance on her for the world. But I think you look too seriously at it. You're such a grave, steady fellow, you don't understand the temptation to such trifling. Besides, you know I am going away immediately, so I shan't make any more mistakes of the kind. So let us say good-night, and talk no more about the matter. The whole thing will soon be forgotten." (*starts to go*)

ADAM—"No! No! It'll not be soon forgotten, as you've come in between her and me, when she might ha' loved me—it'll not be soon forgotten as you've robbed me o' my happiness, while I thought you was my best friend, and a noble-minded man as I was proud to work for. You've meant nothing, have you? I've never kissed her i' my life, but I'd ha' worked hard for years for the right to kiss her. And you make light of it. You think little o' doing what may damage other folks so as you get your bit o' trifling as means nothing. I throw back your favors, for you're not the man I took you for. I'll never count you my friend any more. I'd rather you'd act as my enemy, and fight me where I stand—it's all the amends you can make. (ADAM *throws off his coat and hat, blind with passion, while* ARTHUR *stands pale and motionless, his hands thrust in his pockets.*) What! won't you fight me like a man? You know I won't strike you while you stand so."

ARTHUR—"Go away, Adam—I don't want to fight you."

ADAM—"No, you don't want to fight me; you think I'm a common man as you can injure without answering for it."

ARTHUR—"I never meant to injure you. I didn't know you loved her."

ADAM—"But you've made her love you. You're a double-faced man. I'll never believe a word you say again."

ARTHUR—"Go away, I tell you, or we shall both repent."

ADAM—"No, I won't go away wi'out fightin' you. Do you want provoking any more? I tell you you're a coward and a scoundrel and I despise you!" (AR-THUR *clinches his right hand and deals a blow which sends* ADAM *staggering backward, the two men fight fiercely, twilight deepens.* ADAM *finally gives* ARTHUR *a blow from which he falls and lays motionless.* ADAM *waits for* ARTHUR *to rise.*)

ADAM—"Why don't you get up like a man? I say why don't you get up? (*pause, kneels beside* ARTHUR *and raises his head.*) Have I killed him? Captain! Captain! Dead!—Oh, what have I done by fightin'? taken his life but not changed the past,—Hetty—He breathes. (*gently he loosens* ARTHUR'S *cravat*) Do you feel any pain, sir? (*pause.*) Do you feel any hurt, sir?"

ARTHUR (*puts his hand to his waistcoat,* ADAM *unbuttons it,* ARTHUR *takes a long breath, then replies faintly*)—"Lay my head down, and get me some water if you can." (ADAM *empties tools out of his basket, exits hastily, returns with basket leaking water.*)

ADAM—"Can you drink a drop out o' your hand, sir?" (*kneeling and lifting up* ARTHUR'S *head.*)

ARTHUR—"No, dip my cravat in and souse it on my head." (ADAM *does as requested.*)

ADAM—"Do you feel any hurt inside, sir?"

ARTHUR—"No, no hurt, but rather done up. I suppose I fainted when you knocked me down."

ADAM—"Yes, sir, I'm glad it's no worse."

ARTHUR—"You thought you'd done me, eh? Come, help me on my legs. (*with* ADAM'S *help he rises*) I feel terribly shaky and dizzy. (*leans on* ADAM'S *arm*) That blow of yours must have come against me like a battering ram. I don't believe I can walk alone."

ADAM—"Lean on me, sir; I'll get you along. Will you sit down a bit? You'll perhaps be better in a minute or two."

ARTHUR—"Yes, (*sits in chair beside rustic table*)— Will you go in the Hermitage and get some brandy? You'll see my hunting-bottle somewhere. A leather case with a bottle and glass in it." (ADAM *exits into the Hermitage, quickly returns with the bottle.*)

ADAM—"There's very little brandy in it, sir: (*turning it downward over the glass*) hardly this glass full."

ARTHUR—"Well, give me that." (*he takes a sip or two*)

ADAM—"Hadn't I better run to the Chase and get some more, sir? I can be there and back pretty soon, an' if you don't ha' something to revive you it'll be a stiff walk home for you."

ARTHUR—"No, this will do, I shall soon be up to walking home, now."

ADAM (*hesitatingly*)—"I can't go before I've seen you safe home, sir."

ARTHUR—"No, it will be better for you to stay—sit down." (ADAM *sits on stump, they remain opposite to each other in uneasy silence. They do not look at each other.* ARTHUR *sips the brandy, with visibly renovating effect, presently changes his position to a more comfortable one*)

ADAM—"You begin to feel yourself again, sir?"

ARTHUR—"Yes, but not good for much, rather lazy, and not inclined to move; I'll go home when I've taken this dose." (*pause*)

ADAM—"My temper got the better o' me, and I said things as wasn't true. I'd no right to speak as if you'd know you was doing me an injury; for you'd no grounds for knowing it; I've always kept what I felt for her as secret as I could. (*pause*) And, perhaps, I judged you too harsh—I'm apt to be harsh; and you may ha' acted out o' thoughtlessness more than I should ha' believed was possible for a man wi' a heart and a conscience. We're not all put together alike and sometimes we misjudge one another."

ARTHUR—"Say no more about our anger, Adam, I forgive your momentary injustice; with the exaggerated notions you had in your mind, it was quite natural. We shall be none the worse friends in future I hope because we've fought; you had the best of it, and that was as it should be, for I believe I've been most in the wrong of the two. Come, let us shake hands." (*offers his hand,* ADAM *sits still*)

ADAM—"I don't like to say no, to that, sir, but I can't shake hands till it's clear what we mean by't. I was wrong when I spoke as if you'd done me an injury knowingly, but I wasn't wrong in what I said before, about your behavior t' Hetty, and I can't shake hands wi' you as if I held you my friend the same as ever, till you've cleared that up better." (*pause*)

ARTHUR—"I don't know what you mean by clearing up, Adam. I've told you already that you think too seriously of a little flirtation. But if you are right in supposing there is any danger in it—I'm going away on Saturday to rejoin my regiment, and so there will be an end of it. As for the pain it has given you, I'm heartily sorry for it. I can say no more." (ADAM *rises x's to* R. *looks in silence at the moonlit trees, turns and walks back to* ARTHUR, *standing looking down upon him.*)

ADAM—"Though it's hard work, it will be better for me to speak plain. You see, sir, this isn't a trifle to me, whatever it may be to you. I'm none o' them as can go making love first to one woman and then t' another, and not think it much odds which of 'em I take. What I feel for Hetty's a different sort o' love, such as I believe nobody can know much about but them as feel it. She's more nor everything else to me, all but my conscience and my good name. And if it's true what you've been saying all along—that it's only trifling and flirting, as you call it, that 'ull be put an end to by your going away—why then I'll wait, and hope her heart 'ull turn to me. I'm loath to think you'd speak false to me, and I'll believe your word, however things may look."

ARTHUR—"You would be wronging Hetty more than me not to believe it—(*starting up violently and then sinking back into the chair*)— You seem to forget that in suspecting me, you are casting imputations upon her."

ADAM—"Nay, sir, nay; things don't lie level between Hetty and you. Whatever you may do, you're acting wi' your eyes wide open; but how do you know what's been in her mind? She's all but a child—as any man wi' a conscience in him ought to feel bound to take care on. And whatever you may think, I know you've disturbed her mind. I know she's been fixing her heart on you; for there's many things clear to me now, as I didn't understand before. But you seem to make light o' what she may feel—you don't think o' that." (*x's to* L.)

ARTHUR—"Confound it, Adam, let me alone! I feel it enough without your worrying me."

ADAM—"Well, then, if you feel it, if you feel it as you may ha' put false notions into her mind, an' made her believe as you loved her, when all the while you meant nothing, I've this demand to make o' you—I'm not speaking for myself, but for her. I ask you t' undeceive her before you go away. Y' aren't going away forever, and if you leave her behind wi' a notion in her head o' your feeling about her the same as she feels about you, she'll be hankering after you an' the mischief may get worse. It may be a smart to her now, but it'll save her pain i' th' end."

ARTHUR—"Well, (*impatiently*) what do you want me to do?"

ADAM—"I ask you to write her a letter; tell her the truth, an' take blame to yourself for behavin' as you'd no right to behave. I speak plain, sir. But I can't speak any other way. There's nobody can take care o' Hetty i' this matter but me."

ARTHUR—"I shall do what I think needful without giving promises to you. I shall take what measures I think proper."

ADAM—"No, that won't do—I must know what ground I'm treading on. I must be safe as you've put an end to what ought never to ha' been begun. I don't forget what's owing to you as a gentleman, but in this thing I can't give up to you, we're man to man."

ARTHUR (*pause*)—"I'll see you to-morrow—I can bear no more now, I'm ill." (*rising*)

ADAM—"You won't see her again? (*going close to him*) Either tell me she can never be my wife—tell me you've been lying—or else promise me what I've asked."

ARTHUR—"I promise you; let me go."

ADAM—"When will you write that letter?"

ARTHUR—"To-morrow."

ADAM—"No, now!"

ARTHUR—"Oh, very well." (*impatiently sinking back into his chair and leaning his head upon his hand*) 'Get a candle. You'll find one in the Hermitage—on the shelf over the fireplace. And writing materials on the table. (*exit* ADAM *into Hermitage, returns with lighted candle, pen, paper.* ARTHUR *sits listlessly for a moment, then begins to write.* ADAM *walks silently about, then sits* L. *After a moment* ADAM *rises, picks up his tools and replaces them in the basket. Goes back and sits down with his head buried in his hands. When* ARTHUR *finishes the letter he seals it and hands it to* ADAM) There is the letter, I have written everything you wish. Before you deliver it, ask yourself whether you are not taking a course which may pain her more than if I were to keep silent. (*rising*) There is no need for our seeing each other again. We shall meet with better feelings some months hence." (*going* R.)

ADAM—"You're not well enough to walk alone, sir. Take my arm again."

ARTHUR (*haughtily*)—"I believe I'll not trouble

you. It's getting late and I must be going, or there may be an alarm set up about me at home."

ADAM—"You won't let me go with you, sir?"

ARTHUR—"No."

ADAM—"Very well—good-night, sir. (ARTHUR *exits* R. *without replying*) Perhaps he's i' the right on't not to see me again. It's no use meeting to say more hard words, and it's no use meeting to shake hands and say we're friends again. We're not friends, and it's better not to pretend it. I can't feel the same toward him. God help me. I don't know whether I feel the same toward anybody; I seem as if I'd been measuring my work from a false line and had got it all to measure o'er again." (*puts basket of tools on stick over his shoulder and exits* L.)

End of scene first, act third.

ACT THIRD. SCENE SECOND.

THE HALL FARM.   (NEXT DAY.)   THE KITCHEN.

Same set as Act first.

Discovered, HETTY *and* MOLLY. HETTY *has a basket on her arm.*

MOLLY—"Your arms look like a fine lady's, Hetty, but fine ladies doosna ha' brown hands, for they doosna work, so they keep their hands white. But—maybes thee 'ull ha' white hands, too, someday."

HETTY—"What do you mean?"

MOLLY—"I means that thee'st caught th' fancy o' th' young squire."

Hetty—"Who says so?"

Molly—"Nobody ha' said so, but hanna I got eyes? and canna I see? I am na' blind. Thee knows as he's a takin' notice o' thee."

Hetty—"Well, what o' that?"

Molly—"Oh, I ha'na jealousy, that are'na i' my nature, jealousy are'na, but I doos take notice. Will yez let me come an see thee when thee's a great lady livin' i' the Chase?"

Hetty—"How you talk."

Molly—"If thee wast dressed up, thee'd make a grander lookin' lady nor any I've iver seen visitin' at the Chase."

Hetty—"Molly."

Molly—"Yis, ye would. (*undertone*) If the squire axes thee to marry him on th' sly, 'udn't thee do it?"

Hetty—"Maybe."

Molly—"Course you 'ud—Didn't Meester James marry Sir Lawton's niece an' nobody found it out till it war o' no use to be mad about it? (*pause*) An' then thee'll wear feathers i' thy hair, an' thee'll dress up ivery day in a grand silk frock, as thee's been a-tellin' me Miss Lydia do. An' some days thee'll wear a white 'un an' some days thee'll wear a pink 'un. An' then thee'll ride by the Hall Farm in a coach, an' I'll be on th' lookout, an' when thee sees me thee'll say, 'Good-day, Molly; I hope thee'st well?' An' I'll say (*courtesies*) 'Yis, thank ye, me lady.'"

Hetty—"Think what Aunt Poyser 'ud say, Molly."

Molly—"Aye, she'd scold to see thy feathers noddin' from th' coach window, but what o' that, thee'st not hear it."

(*Voice of* Mrs. Poyser *heard calling from the garden,* "Hetty! Hetty!" *Both girls jump,* Molly *goes into dairy and* Hetty *goes hastily toward the garden door Upper* R., *meets* Mr. *and* Mrs. Poyser *as they enter door Upper* R.)

Mrs. Poyser—"What hast been up to, Hetty? Look at the clock, do; a fine time o' day to begin pickin' the

fruit. (*exit* HETTY *into garden*) She's no better than
a peacock as 'ud strut about on the wall and spread its
tail when the sun shone; there's nothing seems to gi'
her a turn i' th' inside, not even when we thought
Totty had tumbled into the pit. It's my belief her
heart's as hard as a pibble." (*comes down* L.)

POYSER—"Nay, nay, (*sits* R.) thee mustna judge
Hetty too hard. Them young gells air like th' unripe
grain—they'll make good meal by and by, but they're
squashy yit. Thee't see. Hetty'll be all right when
she's got a good husband an' children of her own."

MRS. POYSER—"I don't want to be hard upo' th' gell.
An' let be what may, I'd strive to do my part by a niece
o' yours, an' that I've done; for I've taught her everything as belongs to a house, an' I've told her her duty
often enough, though I've no breath to spare, an' that
catchin' pain comes on dreadful by times. Wi' them
three gells i' th' house, I'd need have twice the strength
to keep 'em up to their work. It's like havin' roast
meat at three fires; as soon as you've basted one, another's burnin'."

Enter MOLLY *from dairy excitedly.*

MOLLY—"O, missus!"

MRS. POYSER—"Well, what is't ails thee gell? Out
with it, what hast happened, hast broke th' churn?"

MOLLY—"No, missus, but old Squire Donnithorne
ha' just drove in at th' gate."

MRS. POYSER—"Squire Donnithorne! Poyser, I'll lay
my life he's brewin' some nasty turn against us, old
Harry doesna call to see us for nothin'."

Enter SQUIRE DONNITHORNE R. C.

SQUIRE DONNITHORNE (*he is short-sighted and
peers at people when talking*)—"Good-day, Mrs. Poyser."

MRS. POYSER—"Your servant, sir." (*courtesies*)

There is much less risk in dairy-land than corn-land."

POYSER (*after a pause, to* MRS. POYSER)—"What dost say?"

MRS. POYSER—"Say? Why, I say you may do as you like about givin' up any o' your corn-land, afore your lease is up, which it won't be for a year come next Michaelmas Lady-day, but I'll not consent to take more dairy work into my hands, either for love or money; an' there's nayther love nor money here, as I can see, on'y other folk's love o' theirselves, an' the money as is to go into other folk's pockets. I know there's them as is born t' own the land, an' them as is born to sweat on't, and I know it's Christian folk's duty to submit to their betters as fur as flesh an' blood 'ud bear it; but I'll not make a martyr o' myself and wear myself to skin an' bone, an' worret myself as if I was a churn wi' butter a-comin' in't, for no landlord in England, nor if he were King George himself!" (*comes down* L.)

SQUIRE—"No, no, my dear Mrs. Poyser, certainly not; you must not overwork yourself; but don't you think your work will rather be lessened than increased in this way? There is so much milk required at the Chase that you will have little increase of cheese and butter making from the addition to your dairy."

POYSER—"Aye, that's true."

MRS. POYSER (*x's back to* L. C.)—"I daresay, I daresay it's true for men as sit i' th' chimney-corner an' make believe as iverything's cut wi' ins an' outs to fit int' iverything else. If you could make a pudding wi' thinking o' th' batter, it 'ud be easy gettin' dinner."

SQUIRE—"I believe selling the milk is the most profitable way of disposing of dairy produce, is it not?"

MRS. POYSER—"How do I know whether the milk 'ud be wanted constant? An' if it wasn't, I'd have to lie awake nights wi' twenty gallons o' milk on my mind! An' there's the fetchin' an' carryin' as 'ud be well half a day's work for a man an' horse,—that's to be took out o' th' profits, I reckon? But there's folks 'ud hold a sieve under the pump and expect to carry away water."

Squire—"That difficulty, about the fetching and carrying, you will not have, Mrs. Poyser. Bethell will do that regularly with the cart and pony."

Mrs. Poyser—"O, sir, begging your pardon, I've niver been used t' havin' gentlefolk's servants comin' about my kitchen a-makin' love to th' gells, an' keepin' 'em wi' their hands on their hips when they should be down on their knees a-scourin'. If we're to go to ruin, it shanna be wi' havin' our back kitchen turned into a public!"

Squire—"Well, Poyser, (*ignoring* Mrs. Poyser.) I can easily make another arrangement about supplying my house. And I shall not forget your readiness to accommodate me. I know you will be glad to renew your lease when the present one expires; otherwise, I daresay, Thurle, who is a man of some capital, would be glad to take both farms, as they can be worked so well together."

Poyser—"I'm sorry, sir, but,—"

Mrs. Poyser—"Then, sir, if I may speak, and I've a right to speak, though I am a woman, for I make one quarter o' th' rent an' save the other quarter,— I say if Mr. Thurle's so ready to take farms under you, it's a pity but what he should take this, an' see if he likes to live in a house wi' all the plagues o' Egypt in't —rats an' mice gnawin' every bit o' cheese, an' runnin' over our heads as we lie i' bed till we expect 'em to eat us up alive,—and it's a mercy they hanna eat the children long ago! I should like to see if there's another tenant beside my husband, as 'ud put up wi' niver havin' a bit o' repairs done till a place tumbles down, an' not then, on'y wi' beggin' an' prayin', an' havin' to pay half. (Squire *going toward door* R. C.) You may run away from my words, sir, an' go spinnin' underhand ways o' doin' us a mischief, but I tell you for once as we're not dumb creatures to be abused and

made money on by them as a' got th' lash i' their
hands. If I'm th' only one as speaks my mind, there's
plenty o' th' same way o' thinkin' i' th' parish, for your
name's no better than a brimstone match in everybody's nose,—if it isna two or three old folks as you
think o' savin' your soul by givin' 'em a bit of flannel
and a drop o' porridge. You may be right i' thinking
it'll take but little to save your soul, for it'll be the
smallest savin' y' iver made, wi' all your scratchin'!"

Exit SQUIRE DONNITHORNE R. C. POYSER *watches
him go, then turns to his wife.*

POYSER—"Thee's done it, now."
MRS. POYSER—"Yes, I know I've done it, but I've
had my say out. There's no pleasure i' livin', if you're
to be corked up foriver and dribble your mind out by
the sly, like a leaky barrel."
POYSER—"I'm sorry thee wast so harsh, Rachel."
MRS. POYSER—"I shan't repent saying what I think,
if I live to be as old as th' old squire, an' there's a
little likelihood,—for it seems as if them as arena
wanted i' this world are the only ones as arena wanted
i' th' next."
POYSER—"But thee wotna like moving from th' old
place and going into a strange parish, where thee
know'st nobody. It'll be hard upo' us both, and upo'
father, too."
MRS. POYSER—"It's no use worretin'; there's plenty
o' things may happen between this an' Michaelmas
twelvemonth. For what we know, th' captain may be
master afore then." (*exit into dairy*)
POYSER—"I am none for worretin', (*getting his
pipe*) but I should be loath to leave th' old place,
an' the parish where I was born and bred and father
afore me. We should leave our roots behind us, I
doubt and never thrive again." (*exit door* L.)

(*Enter* HETTY *from garden* UPPER R. *with basket*

filled with currants. She places basket on table L. *and turns to see* ADAM BEDE *standing in the door* R. C. HETTY *starts.*)

ADAM—"I frightened you. (*entering*) I'm sorry. You've been picking currants?"

HETTY—"Yes, aunt wanted some for pies."

ADAM—"Hetty, I've something particular I'd like to talk to you about."

HETTY—"Very well." (*sits* R. *of table* L.)

ADAM—"I hope you won't think me making too free, but, after what I saw on Thursday night, there's something I want to say to you. You are young, Hetty, and y' haven't seen much o' what goes on i' th' world, and it's right for me to do what I can to save you from harm, for want o' your knowing where you're being led to. If anybody besides me was to see you wi' Captain Donnithorne they'd speak light on you; and besides that, you'll have to suffer yourself wi' giving your love to a man as can never marry you an' take care of you all your life."

HETTY—"You've no right to say as I love him."

ADAM—"I doubt it must be so, Hetty, for I canna believe you'd let any man kiss you and give you a gold locket with his hair in it, and meet him in the grove, if you didn't love him. I'm not blaming you, for I know it 'ud begin by little and little, till at last you'd not be able to throw it off. It's him I blame for stealing your love, when he knew he could never make you the right amends. He's been trifling with you, Hetty, and making a plaything of you and caring nothing about you, as a man ought to care."

HETTY—"Yes, he does care for me; I know better nor you."

ADAM—"Nay, Hetty, if he'd cared for you rightly, he'd never ha' behaved so. He told me himself he meant nothing by his kissing and his presents, and he wanted to make me believe as you thought light of 'em, too. But I know better nor that. I can't help

thinking as you've been trusting t's loving you well
enough to marry you for all he's a gentleman. But
the thought o' marrying you has never entered his
head.",

HETTY—"How do you know? How durst you say
so?"

ADAM—"Perhaps, you don't believe me, Hetty,
maybe you think too well of him—maybe you think
he loves you better than he does. But I've got a letter
in my pocket, that after he told me he meant nothing
I asked him to write to you. I've not read the letter,
but he says he's told you the truth in it. (*takes letter
from his pocket*) Don't let it take too much hold on
you. It would ha' been a mad thing if he'd wanted
to marry you; it 'ud ha' come to no happiness i' the
end. (*she puts out her hand for the letter; ADAM continues to hold it*) Don't bear me ill-will, Hetty, because I'm the means o' bringing you this pain. God
knows I'd ha' borne a good deal worse for the sake o'
sparing it you. (*gives her the letter*) There's nobody
but me knows about this and you needn't fear as any
one 'ull ever hear it from me. I'll take care o' you,
for you're the same as ever to me. I don't believe
you've done any wrong knowingly. If you was being
courted by a man as 'ud make you his wife, and I'd
known you was fond o' him, I should ha' had no right
to speak, but I was bound to interfere when the captain said he'd no thought o' marrying you. You must
ha' seen for some time, Hetty, that I've been in love
wi' you, but there's no use o' my thinking any more
o' that. (*x's to* R.)

(*Enter* TOTTY *from dairy.*)

ADAM—"Hey, Totty! And how is Totty to-day?
(*catches her in his arms and kisses her*) What a fine,
big girl you're getting to be. Would Totty like to ride
on my shoulder—ever so high—and almost touch the
top o' the trees?" (TOTTY *nods her head,* ADAM *puts*

the child on his shoulder and exits Upper R. TOTTY *laughing with delight.*)

(HETTY *looks cautiously about, then sits* R. *of table* L., *opens letter and reads aloud with some difficulty.*)

DEAREST HETTY:

I spoke truly when I said that I loved you. But I ought not to have done as I have and I must do what is right from now on. I would be marrying out of my station if I were to make you my wife. Since I cannot do this, we must part; try not to think about me any more. I am miserable while I write this. Be angry, sweet one; I deserve it. When this reaches you I shall be in Windsor—below is my address—do not write unless there is something I can really do for you. Forgive me and try to forget everything about me, except that I shall be as long as I live,

Your affectionate friend,
ARTHUR DONNITHORNE.

(HETTY *leans her head upon her hand. After a moment she brushes pettishly, some tears away, rises, x's to* R. *crumples letter in her hand.*)

(*Enter* MARTIN POYSER L. *still smoking his pipe.*)

HETTY—"Uncle, will you let me go and be a lady's-maid?"

POYSER—"Why, lass, what ails thee? What's put that into thy head?" (*sits* R. HETTY *x's to* L.)

HETTY—"I should like it better nor farm-work."

POYSER—"Nay, nay; you fancy so because you donna know it, my lass. It wouldna be half so good for your health nor for your luck i' life."

HETTY—"I donna care."

POYSER—"I'd like you to stay wi' us till you've got a good husband; you're my own niece and I wouldna ha' you go to service as long as I ha' got a home for you."

HETTY—"I like the needle-work, and I should get good wages."

POYSER—"Has your aunt been a bit cross wi' you? You mustna mind that, my lass—she does it for thy good. There isna many as are no kin to thee, 'ud ha' done by you as she has."

HETTY—"No, it isn't aunt, but I should like the work better."

POYSER—"It was all very well for you to learn the work a bit, an' I gev' my consent to that fast enough, sin' Mrs. Pomfret was willin' to teach you. But I niver meant you to go to service, my lass; my family's eat their own bread as fur back as anybody knows, an' I wouldna like my niece to take wage now. Besides, Hetty, you've got a good chance o' gettin' a solid, sober husband, as any gell i' this country. (HETTY *begins to cry.*) Hey! hey! don't let's have any cryin'. Cryin's for them as ha' got no home."

HETTY—"Uncle, please let me go."

POYSER—"Nay, my lass, give over cryin'. I'll do better for you nor lettin' you go for lady's-maid."

HETTY—"I'm tired o' allays stayin' here."

POYSER—"I canna make out why you should want to go away, it looked o' late as you'd a mind t' Adam Bede."

HETTY—"Uncle, maybe by and by you'll let me go?"

POYSER—"Nay, till thee'st married, thee must stay wi' us. I know what is best for thee, lass. And so let us hear no more on't." (MR. POYSER *exits into dairy.*)

(HETTY *sits* R. *of table* L., *takes letter from pocket, reads part of it again, bursts out crying.*)

(*Enter* ADAM *and* TOTTY *Upper* R. ADAM *puts* TOTTY *down and she runs off into the dairy.* ADAM *looks at* HETTY.)

ADAM—"Poor child. It's because she's had her first

heartache. I doubt if he will ever suffer so. (*going to her*) Try to bear up under it, Hetty. You mustna give way to your feelings, for if you do you'll look white and ill and your aunt may take notice of it. Thee'st a good friend in me allays, Hetty. (HETTY *puts out her left hand; * ADAM *takes it in his right, and presses her arm close against his heart*)—(*pause.*) I'm going to tell your uncle some news that'll surprise him, Hetty; and I think you'll be glad to hear it, too."

HETTY (*whispering*)—"What's that?"

ADAM—"Why, Mr. Burge has offered me a share in his business, and I'm going to take it."

HETTY—"I'm glad o' that."

ADAM—"I thought you'd be glad, Hetty."

HETTY—"And maybe some day you'll be marryin' Mary Burge?"

ADAM—"No, I shall never marry, unless—to thee. Dost think by and by you could come to care for me in that way, Hetty?" (HETTY *looks up in his face smiling faintly through her tears.*)

HETTY—"Maybe."

ADAM—"Will you try and think as some day you'll marry me?"

HETTY—"I'll marry you any time you say, Adam." (*she puts her round cheek against * ADAM'S *face*)

ADAM—"Hetty! You mean it? I may tell your aunt and uncle?"

HETTY—"Yes."

(*Enter * MR. *and * MRS. POYSER *from dairy * L. C.)

ADAM—"Mr. Poyser, I've just been a-tellin' Hetty, here, that Mr. Burge has offered me a share in his business and that I'm going to take it."

POYSER—"Good, Adam, good! that's as it should be. I wish thee all the success that thee deserves. And that's considerable i' my opinion." (*shakes hands with * ADAM)

MRS. POYSER—"If everybody got their just deserts

i' this world, there'd be few lookin' forrard to a soft
seat i' th' Hereafter."

ADAM—"In a few months time if all goes well, I
can afford to get married, and Hetty has just promised to be my wife. I hope you've no objections
against me for her husband? I'm a poor man as yet,
but she shall want nothing as I can work for."

POYSER—"Objections? What objections can we ha'
to you, lad?"

MRS. POYSER—"Never mind your being poorish;
there's money in your headpiece as there's money i'
th' sown field, but it must ha' time."

POYSER—"You've got enough to begin on, and we
can do a deal tow'rt the bit o' furniture you'll want.
Thee's got feathers and linen to spare—plenty, eh?"

MRS. POYSER—"It 'ud be a poor tale, if I hadna
feathers and linen, when I never sell a fowl but what's
plucked, and the wheels a-going ivery day o' the week."

POYSER—"Come, lass, come and kiss us and let us
wish you luck. (HETTY *goes quietly and kisses her
uncle.*) There, (*putting her on the back*) go and kiss
your aunt. I'm as wishful t' ha' you settled well as if
you was my own daughter; (HETTY *kisses* MRS. POY-
SER) and so's your aunt, for she's done by you this
seven year as if you'd been her own. (HETTY *goes to
sit down.*) Come, come, Adam wants a kiss, too, I'll
warrant, and he's a right to one now. Come, Adam,
take one, else y' arena half a man. (ADAM *blushing
puts his arm around* HETTY, *stoops and gently kisses
her.*) Rachel, we mun ha' some wine to drink their
health."

MRS. POYSER—"Aye, presently." (*exits* L. C. *going* L.)

POYSER—"Hast thee thought of a house for thysen'?
There's none empty i' th' village a'side the little 'un
next to Will Maskery's."

ADAM—"That house would be too small, Mr. Poyser."

POYSER—"Maybe. The best plan 'ud be for thy

mother an' Seth to move there and leave the old home to thee."

ADAM—"Nay, I'd not consent to that. Mother 'ud never be happy but in the old place. Hetty, for my sake you'd be willing mother should live wi' us, wouldn't you?"

HETTY—"Yes—I'd as soon she lived with us as not."

POYSER—"Well spoken, lass. But we needna fix ivery thing to-day. You canna think o' getting married afore Easter at the earliest. (*enter* MRS. POYSER L. C. *with tray and glasses filled with wine*) I'm not for long courtships, but there mun be a bit o' time to make things comfortable."

MRS. POYSER—"Aye, Christian folks can't be married like cukoos, I reckon." (*passes glass of wine to each*)

POYSER—"I'm a bit daunted though when I think as we may ha' notice to quit, and be forced to take a farm twenty miles off."

MRS. POYSER—"I tell thee, Poyser, not t' fret aforehand."

POYSER—"Aye, mayhappen th' captain 'ull come home afore then and make our peace wi' th' old squire. I build upo' that, for I know th' captain 'ull see folks right if he can. But come, drink. May Hetty, (*looking at* ADAM) make you a good and faithful wife, and may Adam, (*looking at* HETTY) make you an honorable, lovin' husband, and may God bless you both." (*all touch glasses and drink.*)

CURTAIN.

ACT FOURTH. SCENE FIRST.

THE RECTORY. EIGHT MONTHS LATER. EVENING.

Same Set as Act First.

Enter REV. ADOLPHUS IRWINE L. C. *followed by* CARROL *who assists the rector to remove his coat, etc.*

CARROL—"Your reverence."
REV. IRWINE—"Well, Carrol?"
CARROL—"Squire Donnithorne is dead."
REV. IRWINE—"What!"
CARROL—"He was found dead in his bed at ten o'clock this morning. Mrs. Irwine begs you will not retire without seeing her. She told me to say that she should be awake when you came home."

(*Enter* MRS. IRWINE L. C. *robed in a dressing gown.*)

MRS. IRWINE—"Well, Dauphin, you're home at last. (*kisses him*) I suppose Carrol has told you the news, that the squire was found dead in his bed this morning?" (*exit* CARROL)
REV. IRWINE—"Yes, mother."
MRS. IRWINE—"So the old gentleman's low spirits and his sending for Arthur, really meant something." (*she sits by fire* L. REV. IRWINE R. *of desk* C.)
REV. IRWINE—"What have they done about Arthur? Sent a message to await him at Liverpool?"
MRS. IRWINE—"Yes, word was sent to him before the news was brought to us."

REV. IRWINE—"Ah, then the message reached him some hours ago; barring delays he should arrive home by midnight."

MRS. IRWINE—"Dear Arthur, I shall live now to see him master at the Chase and making good times on the estate, like a generous-hearted fellow as he is. He'll be as happy as a king now. (REV. IRWINE *sighs.*) What are you so dismal about, Dauphin? Is there any bad news? Or are you thinking of the danger for Arthur in crossing that frightful Irish channel?"

REV. IRWINE—"No, mother, I'm not thinking of that."

MRS. IRWINE—"You've been worried about this law business that you've been to Stoniton about. What in the world is it that you can't tell me?"

REV. IRWINE—"You will know by and by, mother."

MRS. IRWINE—"What a mysterious boy you are. (*rising x's to kiss him*) If you were not such a confirmed bachelor, I should fancy you were in love. But, good-night, my son, after your long ride you must be fatigued. Promise me you will go to bed at once?"

REV. IRWINE—"Presently, mother."

MRS. IRWINE—"Ah, your presentlys, I know them; you're likely to sit up half the night." (*going* L. C.)

REV. IRWINE—"Good-night, mother. (*goes with her to the door; they kiss;* MRS. IRWINE *exits* L. C.) It's no use, it's no use of my going to bed—I can't sleep, with the face of that child, Hetty Sorrel, haunting me."

(*Enter* CARROL L. C.)

REV. IRWINE—"Well, Carrol?"

CARROL—"Adam Bede is in the hall; he says he wishes to see you on particular business, or he wouldn't trouble you, sir. (*pause*) Shall I show him in?"

REV. IRWINE—"Yes, Carrol."

(CARROL *exits* L. C. *then returns and shows in* ADAM BEDE.)

Rev. Irwine—"Good-evening, you want to speak to me, Adam? Sit down. (Rev. Irwine *sits* R. *of desk* C. *and points* Adam *to a chair opposite him.*)

Adam—"I come to you, sir, as the gentleman I look up to most of anybody in the world."

Rev. Irwine—"I am gratified to hear you say that, Adam."

Adam—"I've something very painful to tell you— something as it'll pain you to hear as well as me to tell. (Mr. Irwine *nods his head slowly.*) You wast' ha' married me and Hetty Sorrel, you know, sir, o' th' fifteenth o' this month. I thought she had come to love me, and I was th' happiest man i' the parish. But a dreadful blow's come upon me. She's gone away, sir, and we don't know where. (Mr. Irwine *starts up as if involuntarily, but controls himself. Walks to the window* R. *and draws curtains, then returns to his seat.*) She said she was going to visit Dinah Morris at Snowfield, and I went to fetch her back, but she'd never been there. I'm going a long journey to look for her, and I can't trust to anybody but you, where I'm going."

Rev. Irwine—"Have you no idea of the reason she went away?"

Adam—"It's plain enough she didna want to marry me, sir. She didna like it when it came so near. But that isna all, I doubt; there's somebody else as is concerned in this besides me. (Adam *looks on the floor, pauses, then lifts his head and looks straight at* Mr. Irwine.) You know the man I've reckoned my greatest friend and used to be proud to think as I should pass my life i' working for him?" (Mr. Irwine, *as if self-control has forsaken him, grasps* Adam's *arm which rests on the table.*)

Rev. Irwine—"No, Adam, no, don't say it, don't! (*relaxing his hold.*) Go on—I must hear it."

Adam—"That man behaved to Hetty as he'd no right to behave to a girl in her station o' life. Just before he went away I found him a-kissing her as they were parting in the grove. There'd been nothing said between me and Hetty, then, though I'd loved her for a long while and she knew it. But I reproached him with his actions, and blows passed between us; and he said solemnly to me after that, as it had been all nonsense, and no more than a bit o' flirting. I asked him to write a letter and tell Hetty he'd meant nothing, for I saw clear enough by things as I hadna understood at the time, as he'd got hold of her heart. I gave Hetty the letter, and she seemed to bear up after awhile better than I'd expected—and she behaved kinder and kinder to me—maybe she didna know her own feelings then, and they came back upon her when it was too late—I don't want to blame her—I can't think as she meant to deceive me. But I was encouraged to think she loved me—and—you know the rest, sir. (*aroused*) It's on my mind as he's been false to me, and 'ticed her away, and she's gone to him—and I'm going now to see; I can't go back to work till I know what's become of her." (MR. IRWINE *places his hand upon* ADAM'S *arm this time gently.*)

REV. IRWINE—"Adam, my dear friend, you have had hard trials in your life. And you have proven that you can bear sorrow manfully, as well as act manfully: both tasks are required at our hands. And now there is a heavier sorrow coming upon you than any you have yet known. (MR. IRWINE *hesitates.*) I have seen Hetty this morning. (ADAM *springs up.*) She is not gone to him. She is in Stoniton."

ADAM—"She is in Stoniton!" Parson, what——"

REV. IRWINE—"Wait, Adam, wait. (ADAM *sits.*) She is in a very unhappy position, in one that will make it harder for you to find her, my poor friend, than to have lost her, forever."

ADAM (*almost in a whisper*)—"What do you mean? Tell me."

REV. IRWINE—"She has been arrested—She is in prison—Her trial ended to-day."

ADAM—"Her trial! For what?"

REV. IRWINE—"For a great crime—the murder of her child."

ADAM—"It can't be! (*starts for the door, turns, bracing his back against door.*) It isna possible! She isna guilty! Who says it?"

REV. IRWINE—"God grant she may be innocent, Adam."

ADAM—"But who says she's guilty? What do you know about it?"

REV. IRWINE—"Try and be calm, Adam, and I'll tell you. (ADAM *comes back to the table, gradually takes his seat again.*) On Tuesday I received word that a young woman was on trial at Stoniton, who would neither tell who she was nor where she came from. But when she was searched, a small red leather pocket book was found in which two names were written, 'Hetty Sorrel, Hayslope,' and 'Dinah Morris, Snowfield'. As a magistrate, application was made to me for identifying her."

ADAM—"You went to Stoniton?"

REV. IRWINE—"At once. And have been with her until the close of the trial."

ADAM—"Oh, God! (*groaning and leaning on the table. There is a pause, then he jumps up.*) If there's been any crime, it's at his door, not her's. It's his doing. He taught her to deceive; he deceived me first. Let 'em put him on trial. Let him stand beside her in court, and I'll tell how he got hold of her heart and 'ticed her to evil; and then lied to me. Is he to go free, while they lay all the blame on her?—so weak and young. Oh, I can't bear it! It's hard to lay upon me—it's hard to think she's wicked. (*sinks in chair, then sits motionless with eyes fixed.*) It was fear made her hide it—I forgive her for deceiving me—I forgive thee, Hetty—thee wast deceived, too—it's gone hard wi' thee, my poor Hetty—but they'll never make me believe any wrong o' thee. (*pause, then he starts up coming down L.*) I'll go to him—I'll bring him back—I'll make him look at her in her misery—he shall look at her till he can't forget it—it shall follow him till he can't eat nor sleep—he shan't escape wi' lies this time. He shall go to Stoniton if I ha' to drag him there myself." (*goes toward door* L. C.)

Rev. Irwine—"No, Adam, no. The punishment will fall without your aid. He is now on his way home and may arrive at any moment. Besides, Adam, you forget that there are other people to consider as well as yourself. This sorrow has fallen on the good Poysers more heavily than I can bear to think."

Adam—"Have they been to see Hetty?"

Rev. Irwine—"No, Mrs. Poyser is too ill to go, and though Mr. Poyser has spent money liberally in Hetty's defense, he cannot find it in his heart to go to her."

Adam—"Poor child. Such a little while ago looking so happy and so pretty—kissing 'em all, and they wishing her luck—Oh, my poor, poor Hetty—dost think on it now?"

Rev. Irwine—"Drink some wine, (*offering him some wine*) and show me you mean to bear up like a man." (*with quiet obedience* Adam, *drinks a little*)

Adam—"Will you go with me to Stoniton, parson?"

Rev. Irwine—"Yes, of course, I will go with you, Adam."

Adam—"When? To-morrow, first thing i' th' morning?"

Rev. Irwine—"If you wish it, yes."

Adam—"We may meet him if we set out early enough?"

Rev. Irwine—"No, he will come from the opposite direction. The nearest place for him to leave the coach is at Lansdale."

Adam—"Yes—well then, we'll wait—we can't go till I've seen him. She shall ha' justice. I don't care what she's done—it was him brought her to it, and he shall know it—he shall feel it—if there's a just God, that man shall feel what it is t' ha' brought a child like her to misery."

REV. IRWINE—"Adam, if you obey your passion, though you deceive yourself in calling it justice—it will lead you precisely as it has led him; nay, it may lead you into a worse crime."

ADAM—"No, not worse. I don't believe it's worse. I'd sooner do it. I'd sooner do a wickedness as I could suffer for myself, than ha' brought her to do wickedness."

REV. IRWINE—"Adam, there is no wrong deed of which a man can bear the punishment alone. An act of vengeance would only add an evil to those we are already suffering under."

ADAM—"I must see him afore we go to Stoniton."

REV. IRWINE—"But he may not come as we expect. Some accident may delay him for two or three days. I think we would better not wait. Instead, I will send a note to the Chase to be delivered as soon as he reaches home, telling him to follow me to Stoniton."

ADAM—"Would he do it?"

REV. IRWINE—"Yes, if I asked him to, I am confident he would. Such an arrangement would be better than for us to wait here in a state of uncertainty—when we might be of comfort to Hetty. (*watches the effect of his words upon* ADAM) I'll write the note now, and send it off at once. (*pen, ink and paper on table.* ADAM *sits quietly L. of table C. while* REV. IRWINE *writes the letter*)

REV. IRWINE (*writes*) "ARTHUR:
      I send this letter to meet you on your arrival because I may then be at Stoniton, where I am called by the most painful duty it has ever been given me to perform. Hetty Sorrel is in prison under a terrible accusation. The jury are considering the verdict. Follow me to Stoniton at once.
                              ADOLPHUS IRWINE.

REV. IRWINE *folds and seals letter, taps bell.* CARROL *enters L. C.*

ADAM—"Oh, God! and men ha' suffered like this before—(REV. IRWINE *gives* CARROL *directions and he exits*) and poor, helpless young things ha' suffered like her. (*pause*) Tell me what they've said, I must know it now—I must know what they have brought against her. Did the evidence go hard against her? What do you think? Tell me the truth, Mr. Irwine."

REV. IRWINE—"Yes, Adam. The doctor's testimony is heavy against her."

ADAM—"But what did she say?"

REV. IRWINE—"Denied everything from first to last, in the face of the most positive evidence."

ADAM—"It's no use—it's no use, I can't believe she's guilty, parson. (*pause*) How did she look?"

REV. IRWINE—"Frightened. Very frightened, and when they asked her if she'd plead guilty or not guilty, she did not answer, so they plead for her, 'not guilty.'"

ADAM—"Was there nobody there to stand by her? nobody there as 'ud care for her?"

REV. IRWINE—"No one, but me. I sat by her and did what I could for her."

ADAM—"God bless you for it! God bless you for it!"

REV. IRWINE—"It was little that anyone could do, for she sat like a white image, refusing to speak and seeming not to hear nor see."

ADAM—"Poor child. Poor Hetty, my sweet. (*pause*) Has Dinah Morris been to see her?"

REV. IRWINE—"No, they are afraid the letter has not reached her. It seems she is away preaching, and they have no exact address. If she knew the child needed her, I am sure she would go to her."

ADAM—"Aye, that she would. Did you ask Hetty, did you say anything about me, sir?"

REV. IRWINE—"Yes, I asked her if you might come to see her."

ADAM—"Well, parson, well?"

REV. IRWINE—"She is very much changed, Adam, and she shrinks from seeing anyone. When I mentioned your name she only said 'No, no,' in the same cold way."

ADAM (*jumping up and walking about*)—"Oh, she lies there in misery, while he—he——"

REV. IRWINE—"He will suffer long and bitterly. Why do you seek vengeance in this way, Adam? No amount of torture that you could inflict on him would benefit her."

ADAM—"No! (*sinking in chair* L. *of table* C.) that's what makes the blackness of it—it can never be undone. She can never be my sweet Hetty again, looking up at me, the prettiest thing that ever smiled. I thought she loved me—and was good."

(*Enter* CARROL L. C.)

REV. IRWINE—"Well, Carrol?"

CARROL—"There is a messenger in the hall from Stoniton. He says he must see you."

REV. IRWINE—"I will go to him." (*starts to go* L. C.)

ADAM—"No, parson, no. If it's news from her let me hear it, too."

REV. IRWINE—"Very well. Show him in, Carrol." (*exit* CARROL L. C.; *returns showing in a messenger*)

MESSENGER—"Rev. Mr. Irwine?"

REV. IRWINE—"That is my name."

MESSENGER—"You asked to be notified of the verdict in the Sorrel case?"

REV. IRWINE—"I did."

ADAM—"Speak out, man, quick, speak, what is it?"

MESSENGER—"Guilty."

ADAM (*staggering back*)—"Oh! She's not guilty! She's not guilty! You don't think she is, sir, do you? (*exit messenger.*) She can't ha' done it. Will they hang her?"

REV. IRWINE—"We can try for a pardon, Adam. Her youth will be a plea for her."

ADAM—"Come! You promised to go wi' me to Stoniton. I'm going."

Rev. Irwine—"Not to-night."

Adam—"Yes, now! It's cowardly o' me to keep
away a minute longer. I'm going to her, for all she's
been deceitful. We ha' no business to hand folks over
to God's mercy and then forget to show mercy ourselves. I'll go to her, an' I'll stand by her, I'll stand
by her to the end. Come! Mr. Irwine. Come!"
(*grabs up his hat and starts for the door* l. c.)

End of Scene First, Act Fourth.

ACT FOURTH—SCENE SECOND.

The Prison. (Two Weeks Later.) Early Morning.

The Prison.

Cell door l. Straw pallet r. Chair l. c. Small
window high in wall r.

Discovered, Hetty *seated on straw pallet with her
face buried in her knees. Key turns harshly in the
lock. Enter* Jailor *followed by* Dinah Morris l.

Jailor—"There she is."

Dinah—"Thank thee, friend."

Jailor—"She's so sullen most o' th' time, she won't
answer when she's spoken to. Is she kin o' 'yourn?"

Dinah—"Yea, my own aunt married her uncle. I
was away at Leeds and didn't know of this trouble in
time to get here, before. What hour does the cart set
out?"

Jailor—"Eight o'clock. It's pretty dark in here
now, but it'll be lighter as the sun gets up. (*going*) If
you want anything, I'll be within call."

DINAH—"I am grateful for thy kindness. (*exit* JAILOR L.*) (*pause*) Hetty, (*slight movement of* HETTY's *frame, but she does not look up*) Hetty,— it's Dinah. (HETTY *raises her head a little as if listening.*) Hetty,—Dinah is come to you. (HETTY *lifts her head slowly and timidly, the two women look into each others faces,* DINAH *stretches out her arms.*) Don't you know me, Hetty? Don't you remember Dinah? Did you think I wouldn't come to you in trouble? (HETTY *looks fixedly on* DINAH's *face, but does not move*)—I'm come to be with you, Hetty,—not to leave you—to stay with you— to be your sister to the last (*slowly* HETTY *rises, takes a step forward and is clasped in* DINAH's *arms—long pause. They sit on pallet.*) Hetty, do you know who it is that sits by your side?"

HETTY—"Yes, it's Dinah."

DINAH—"And do you remember the evening we met in the wood, and I told you to be sure and think of me as a friend in trouble?"

HETTY (*pause*)—"Yes, but you can do nothing for me. You can't make 'em do anything. They'll hang me to-day. It's morning now." (*shudders*)

DINAH—"No, Hetty, I can't save you from that death. But isn't the suffering less hard when you have somebody with you that feels for you, that you can speak to, and say what's in your heart?"

HETTY—"You won't leave me, Dinah? You'll keep close to me?"

DINAH—"No, Hetty, I won't leave you. I'll stay with you to the last—But, Hetty, there is some one else in this place beside me, some one close to you."

HETTY (*frightened whisper*)—"Who?"

DINAH—"Some one who has been with you through all you hours of trouble—one who has known every thought you have had—has seen where you went, where you lay down and rose up again, and all the deeds you have tried to hide in darkness— And to-day, when I can't follow you, when my arms can't reach you, when death has parted us, He, who is with us now, and knows all, will be with you then. It makes no difference whether we live or die, we are in the presence of God."

HETTY—"O, Dinah, won't nobody do anything for me? Will they hang me to-day? —I wouldn't mind if they'd let me live."

DINAH—"My dear Hetty,—death is very dreadful to you, I know. But if you had a friend to take care of you after death, in that other world—some one whose love is greater than mine, who can do everything—If God, our Father was your friend, and was willing to save you from sin and suffering, so as you should neither know wicked feelings nor pain again, if you could believe He loved you and would help you, as you believe I love and will help you, it wouldn't be so hard to die, would it?"

HETTY (*with sullen sadness*)—"But I can't know anything about it."

DINAH—"Because, Hetty, you are shutting up your soul against Him, by trying to hide the truth. God's love and mercy can overcome all things, all things but our willful sin; sin that we cling to and will not give up. You believe in my love for you, don't you, Hetty?"

HETTY—"Yes."

DINAH—"But if you hadn't let me come near you; if you wouldn't have looked at me or spoken to me, you'd have shut me out from helping you. I couldn't have made you feel my love. Don't shut God's love out in that way, by clinging to falsehood and sin, but open your heart to Him, say, 'I have done this great wickedness; O, God, have mercy upon me, and save me.' And then there will enter into your soul light and blessedness and strength and peace. Cast it off now, Hetty, now; confess the wickedness you have done, and have rest. Let us kneel down together, for we are in the presence of God. (*they sink on their knees each holding the other's hand, a pause*) Hetty, we are before God; He is waiting for you to tell the truth."

HETTY—"Dinah—help me—I can't feel anything like you."

DINAH (*pause*)—"Thou, who hast known the depths of all sorrow; Thou, who hast entered that black darkness where God is not, and hast uttered the cry of the forsaken, stretch forth Thy hand, and rescue this, Thy wandering child. The darkness surrounds her, she does not know the way to come to Thee; she can only feel that her heart is hard and she is helpless. She cries to me, Thy weak creature,—Saviour,—it is a blind cry to Thee. Hear it. Pierce the darkness. Look upon her with Thy face of love and melt her hard heart. See, Lord, I bring her in my arms for Thee to heal and bless. Breathe upon her Thy life-giving spirit, and make her feel Thy living presence. Saviour,—it is yet time, snatch this poor soul from darkness. I believe, I believe in Thy infinite love, yea, Lord, I see Thee coming like the morning with healing on Thy wings. Come, mighty Saviour, open her blind eyes, let her see that Thy love dost encompass her. Let her tremble at nothing but at the sin which cuts her off from Thee. Melt her hard heart, unseal her closed lips, and make her cry with her whole soul, 'Father, I have sinned!' "

HETTY (*sobbing and throwing her arms about* DINAH)—"Dinah, I will speak—I will tell—I won't hide it any more. (DINAH *raises her from the floor and they sit on the pallet again, after sobs grow less hysterical—she whispers*) I did do it, Dinah—I left it in the wood and it cried—I heard it cry a long way off—all night—(*the remainder of her speeches* HETTY *should play in a dull monotone*) and I went back be cause it cried. I didn't want to hurt it—but I thought perhaps there might somebody find it. I put it down there because I was so miserable—I didn't know where to go—I tried to kill myself, but I couldn't. And when I went back, it was gone."

DINAH—"Were did you go when you left Hayslope, Hetty?"

HETTY—"To Windsor. I went to find him, as he might take care o' me; and he was gone with the regiment to Ireland, and then I didn't know what to do. I daren't go back home again—I couldn't bear th' scorn o' everybody."

DINAH—"If only you had come to me, Hetty."

HETTY—"I thought o' you sometimes and it was that made me come toward Stoniton, but when I got to Stoniton I began to be afraid, because I was going towards home. And an old beggar woman was kind to me. Oh, it was so dreadful, Dinah. I couldn't bear being so lonely and coming to beg for want. And the thought gave me strength to get up and dress myself. —And when the old woman went out, I put on my bonnet and shawl an' took the baby in my arms an' went out into the dark street. I walked fast, on and on, till it got lighter—the moon came out—O, Dinah! it frightened me when it first looked at me out of the clouds,—it never looked so afore. And I turned out o' the road into the fields, for I was afraid o' meeting somebody. I came to a haystack; there was a place cut into it, where I could make a bed; I crawled in, and went to sleep. When I woke up it was beginning to be light, and I saw some woods close by, and it was so early I thought I could leave the baby there and somebody would find it when I was a long ways off. I wanted to go home, and I thought I'd get rides in carts and go home and tell 'em I'd been to try and see for a place and couldn't get one. I longed for home, Dinah."

DINAH—"Of course you did, my child, and you needed one so much."

HETTY—"By and by, I came to a place where there was lots o' turf, and I sat down to think what I should do. And all of a sudden I saw a hole under a tree and it darted into me as I might put the baby there. So I wrapped it in my shawl an' laid it down. And then

I ran out o' th' wood into the fields, but the crying held
me back; I couldn't go away for all I wanted to go.
And I sat against the haystack to watch if anybody
'ud come; I was hungry and I'd only a bit o' bread
left; but I couldn't go away."

DINAH—"My dear Hetty."

HETTY—"After awhile—hours and hours—the man
came—him in a smock frock, and he looked at me so,
I made haste and went on."

DINAH—"Where did you go then?"

HETTY—"I walked till I came to a village. I was so
sick and faint. I got something to eat, but I was
frightened to stay there for I heard it crying and I
thought the other folks heard it, too. It was getting
dark, and I was so tired, Dinah, but I went on. At
last I saw a barn way off from any house. I got there
and hid myself behind the hay and straw and I went
to sleep. But, O, Dinah! the crying kept waking me,
and I thought that man as looked at me so, was come
and laying hold o' me. I slept a long while and at
last it was morning and I got up and turned back the
way I'd come. I couldn't help it, Dinah, it was the
crying made me go. I forgot about going home, I
couldn't think about anything but the place in the
wood. I see it now. O, Dinah! shall I allays see it?"
(HETTY *clings to* DINAH.)

DINAH—"No, Hetty, no; in a little while all the pain
and the sorrow of it will be gone."

HETTY—"When I got to the place it was empty. I
was like a stone with fear. I couldn't move. I
couldn't run away. I couldn't wish or try for
anything; it seemed as if I should stay there forever and nothing 'ud ever change. But after awhile
some men came and took me away. (*shudders*) O,
Dinah! do you think God will take away that crying
and the place in the wood, now I've told everything?"

(*Enter* JAILOR L.)

DINAH (*going to him*)—"Is it time?"

JAILOR—"No, not yet. Mr. Irwine is outside, he wants to know if she won't let Adam Bede come in wi' him. Adam Bede's been here afore, but she'd never see him."

DINAH (*going to* HETTY)—"Hetty, Mr. Irwine and Adam Bede are waiting to see you—Shall they come in? (HETTY *hesitates, then nods her head.*) Yea, let them come in. (*exit* JAILOR) Hetty, there is no one who has a deeper love for you than Adam Bede—no one on earth to whom you have done a greater wrong; when he comes, be kind to him. Ask him to forgive you. He will, Hetty, for he loves you."

(*Enter* JAILOR *followed by* MR. IRWINE *and* ADAM BEDE L.)

DINAH—"Mr. Irwine. (IRWINE *goes to* HETTY) Be comforted, Adam Bede, the Lord has not forsaken her."

ADAM—"Bless you for coming to her."

DINAH—"Thank thee, friend—Hetty desires to ask your forgiveness. And now the time is short."

ADAM (*walks back and forth*)—"It won't be,—it'll be put off—there'll, perhaps, come a pardon. Mr. Irwine said there was hope; he said that I needn't quite give it up."

DINAH—"That's a blessed thought to me. It's a fearful thing hurrying her soul away so fast. But Divine Love has taken the pride out of her heart and this fills me with trust that God will show her His mercy. You will say good-bye and let her ask your forgiveness?"

ADAM—"I can't, I can't say good-bye while there's hope. I'm listening and listening—I can't think o' anything but that. It can't be as she'll die a shameful death—I can't bring my mind to it."

DINAH—"I will not urge you."

ADAM—"If I could do anything to save her—but t' have to bide still and do nothing. It's hard for a

man to bear—and to think o' what might ha' been now,
if it hadna been for him!"

DINAH—"Aye, *it is* a heavy cross. But remember,
we must learn to rise above sorrow and pain, and then
there may come good out of all this that we don't now
see."

ADAM—"Good come out of it? That doesna alter
th' evil. When a man's spoiled his fellow creature's
life, he's no right to comfort himself wi' thinking
good may come out of it; somebody's good doesna alter
her misery."

(*Enter* JAILOR L.)

JAILOR—"The cart is to set out in five minutes. Visitors must leave the prison."

DINAH (*to* MR. IRWINE)—"You will stay till we go
to the cart?"

REV. IRWINE—"Yes."

ADAM (*to* JAILOR)—"Is there no news come,—no
pardon?" (DINAH *goes to* HETTY.)

JAILOR—"None."

DINAH (*leads* HETTY *to* ADAM. HETTY *rests her
check against* DINAH'S. HETTY *and* ADAM *look at
each other.* HETTY *trembles*)—"Speak to him, Hetty,
tell him what is in your heart."

HETTY (*obeys like a child*)—"Adam—I'm sorry, I
behaved wrong to you—will you— forgive me before
I die?"

ADAM—"Yes,—I forgive thee, Hetty,—I forgave
thee long ago." (HETTY *keeps hold of* DINAH'S *hand
but steps forward a little, timidly.*)

HETTY—"Will you kiss me again, Adam, for all I've
been so wicked?" (ADAM *draws her to him and folds
her in his arms.*) And tell him, tell him—for there's
nobody else to tell him—as I went after him and
couldn't find him—and I hated him and cursed him
once, but Dinah says I should forgive him—and
I try—for else God won't forgive me." (*they separate*)

DINAH (*to* ADAM)—"Farewell; our heavenly Father comfort you and strengthen you to bear all things. (ADAM *presses* DINAH'S *hand and exits* L.) Close your eyes, Hetty, and let us pray without ceasing."

(*Distant noise of shouting heard, shouts come nearer and nearer.*)

HETTY—"What is that, Dinah? Are they coming for me? Oh, save me, Dinah, save me! Can't you save me?"

DINAH—"O, Father, give us strength, for Thou art strength, and we are Thy weak creatures."

(*Noise becomes a tumult,* JAILOR *opens cell door,* ARTHUR DONNITHORNE *rushes in with glazed eyes and carrying a paper in his hand. Falls at* HETTY'S *feet.*)

REV. IRWINE (*taking paper out of his hands*)— "What is this?"

ARTHUR—"Read—to—her—quick, quick!"

REV. IRWINE (*reads*)—"Hetty Sorrel shall be transported to Australia for life and the sentence of death is hereby revoked!" (HETTY *leans upon* MR. IRWINE'S *shoulder in a half-fainting condition.* JAILOR *exits.*)

DINAH (*extending her arms and looking upward*) —"God of mercy, I thank Thee! I thank Thee!" (*outside the cheering of the crowd is heard.*)

CURTAIN.

ACT FIFTH.

INDIA, APRIL 6TH, 1799.   GROVE OF SULTANPÉT.

(SIX MONTHS LATER.)

BATTLE IN PROGRESS.   NOISE OF CANNONADING.

At rise of curtain soldiers, headed by an officer on horseback, are marching across the stage from L. *to* R. *Fife and drum corps. Followed by guns drawn by horses, and a battalion of sepoys. Discovered,* DINAH MORRIS, *bending over a wounded man down* L.

Enter SURGEON MALTBY R.

(DINAH, *rising, x's quickly to him.*)

DINAH—"How is the battle going?"

SURGEON—"If there is no repetition of last night's retreat, Tippu Sahib's forces will soon be routed."

DINAH—"Heaven be praised!"

SURGEON—"With the 94th regiment Colonel Wellesley is doing nobly."

DINAH—"Will there be such a victory as at Malvilli?"

SURGEON—"I trust so. Thus far the number of British killed and wounded is but slight."

DINAH—"God grant it may continue so. How long must this misery go on, doctor?"

SURGEON—"Until Tippu's power is broken, until Seringapatam is taken."

DINAH—"I pray that may be soon."

Enter JACK CRANAGE L.

SURGEON (*to* JACK)—"I shall establish new quarters at this spot and have part of last night's wounded transferred here."

JACK—"Yes, sir."

SURGEON—"This will also be a suitable place to bring some of those injured to-day." (*exit* L.)

DINAH (*aside*)—"Those injured to-day. I cannot think it is needful such suffering should be."

JACK *looks curiously at* DINAH, *approaches her.*

JACK—"I say, miss, was you ever in Hayslope, England?"

DINAH—"Yea, there are those very dear to me living there."

JACK—"I thought I'd seen you afore. You're the little Methody preacher. Don't you remember me? I'm Jack Cranage."

DINAH—"Jack Cranage. Are you Chad Cranage, the blacksmith's son?"

JACK—"That's who I be."

DINAH—"God bless thee, friend. (*offers hand*) I am glad to see thee. What news do you hear from home?"

JACK—"I ha' heard no news o' late an' that's good news. But how'd you get here? how'd they come to let a woman through to the front?"

DINAH—"At first I was forbidden. But when I told them that I saw clearly it was the Lord's will for me to come, they gave me leave. To what regiment do you belong, friend?"

JACK—"To the 94th. I'm detailed to help bring in the wounded."

DINAH—"Then I shall see thee through the day. My work is here beside the surgeon. To what company do you belong?"

JACK—"Company B., Captain Arthur Donnithorne."

DINAH—"Tell me of the young man. Has any harm come to him?"

JACK—"Not's I know of."

DINAH (*aside*)—"Thank God. Then all may yet be well. Have you seen Adam Bede of late?"

JACK—"Yes, I ha' seen him, but he ain't in our company. He's in Company E."

DINAH—"Will you see Adam Bede to-day, think?"

JACK—"Mayhappen, I might see him."

DINAH—"If you should, will you tell him that Dinah Morris is here, that she would like to speak with him?"

JACK—"I ain't likely to see him, but if I do I'll tell him what you say." (*going* R.)

DINAH—"I thank thee, friend."

Noise of cannonading heard in the distance R.

JACK (*looking off* R.)—"They're hard at it. Tippu's men 'ull catch it to-day. Afore Lord Mornington gets through with him Tippu Sahib 'ull wish he'd never made his blasted alliance with the French." (*exit* R.)

Enter SURGEON MALTBY L., *followed by sepoys carrying injured men. Enter three or four native women. They assist* DINAH *in looking after the injured. The firing continues. Uproar increases.*

Enter R. *some British soldiers, forced back by Tippu's men. They fight fiercely. British soldiers force Tippu's men off the stage* R. *Some wounded left on the stage. These* DINAH *and the women care for.*

Enter JACK CRANAGE *and a sepoy* R. *carrying* ADAM BEDE. *He is wounded and unconscious.*

SURGEON—"Place him here. (*indicating* L. C.) Lay him down carefully. (*they lay him down.* SURGEON *examines* ADAM. CRANAGE *stands by*). Poor fellow."

JACK—"He's going to die?"

SURGEON—"Yes, his wound is fatal."

JACK—"An' he needna been hurt at all if he hadna taken what was meant for Captain Donnithorne."

SURGEON—"What's that you say?"

JACK—"Just now, on the field, I was givin' drink to a man who was dyin' when I heard a yell, an' saw Captain Donnithorne fightin' hand to hand wi' some o' those damned Mahrattas. He was gettin' th' worst o' it till Adam Bede sprang up an' ran between 'em. They had an awful tussle an' th' next thing I knew Adam Bede was lying on the ground as if he was dead."

SURGEON—"If you hadn't brought him in at once he never would have left the field alive."

ADAM *recovers consciousness.* JACK *goes to* DINAH.

ADAM—"What ha' happened, Doctor?"

SURGEON—"You've been wounded. Are you in pain?"

ADAM—"It doesna matter about me. Where is Captain Donnithorne?"

SURGEON—"On the field. You saved him. He is unhurt."

ADAM—"It's all square, then—doctor, is it all over wi' me?"

SURGEON—"You are a brave fellow. Take some of this cordial, it will keep up your strength. (ADAM *drinks from flask.*) I will do what I can for you."

ADAM—"I know—I know what you mean, doctor—I ha' got to die."

JACK *and* DINAH *advance.* ADAM *looks at* DINAH *bewilderedly.*

ADAM—"Dinah. Is it you? Is it Dinah Morris?"

DINAH—"Yea, Adam, it is Dinah. (DINAH *kneels on one knee and holds* ADAM *in her arms.*) Lean on me. There, rest on my shoulder."

SURGEON *and* JACK *retire up stage.*

ADAM—"I ha' longed to see you, Dinah."

DINAH—"Thank thee, Adam. And it lightens my heart to see thee, and to hear of the noble deed you have done to-day."

ADAM—"Ah, Dinah, I ha' done no noble deed."

DINAH—"Nay, Adam, but it *is* noble to lay down thy life for one who has injured thee."

ADAM—"But you don't know all—I ha' been a wicked sinner."

DINAH—"Adam, be comforted."

ADAM—"No, no, I mun tell you. You mun hear me —I came to India to follow him."

DINAH—"I know, Adam."

ADAM—"I would ha' followed him to th' ends o' th' earth.—Though I couldna get in his company I enlisted in the same regiment; an' sin' then I've waited, days, weeks, for the chance to kill him."

DINAH—"O, Adam, that sin thou hast atoned for."

ADAM—"If it hadna been for th' disgrace to mother an' Seth, I would ha' killed him in England. But I didna want to make it worse for them, an' I thought in a battle nobody would know how he was shot. Dinah, I was mad to murder him."

DINAH—"Don't, don't speak about it now."

ADAM—"Last night when I heard we was goin' into battle I was happy—for the first time sin' so long ago. I could hardly wait for th' break o' day. I was all fever- ish an' afraid as somethin' might happen to me so as I'd miss my chance. I kep' sayin' to myself, To-morrow, to-morrow, O, God, let me ha' all my senses until to- morrow. Let me live just one day more.—Toward mornin' I fell asleep—I dreamed o' home, o' you, Dinah, an' you was bendin' over me just as you are now, your face lookin' so lovin' an' sorrowful."

DINAH—"I was praying for thee, then. It was shown to me that thou must wrestle as Jacob wrestled, and I prayed for thee as I had never prayed for any one before."

ADAM—"When I woke up it was mornin' an' time

to march. As we fell in I could hear you sayin' just
as plain, Adam, for my sake, for your own sake, forgi'e
him. But I answered, No, no, he shall be punished.
I ha' th' right to kill him.—We went into battle.
I watched him. I came closer an' closer. I
took aim. Dinah, you mun ha' been prayin' then, for I
heard a voice that would be answered say to me, Who
are you? Ha' you never done wrong? What right
ha' you to take this man's life? I dropped my gun an'
stood pantin' as if I'd been runnin' an' was out of
breath. Somethin' held me back; I tried, but I couldna
lift the gun. Just then I saw the captain was fightin'
alone wi' two tall men. He was gettin' th' better o'
them till more came up. They were shoutin' an' wavin'
their crooked swords an' I knew it meant death to go in
between 'em, but I didna think o' that. I forgot everythin', everythin', Dinah, but I mun save th' captain's
life. An' I ha' saved his life, an' it's all over wi' me.—
But I forgi'e him, Dinah, I forgi'e him, an' I ha' no
more hard feelin's toward him."

DINAH—"O, God! Thou hast saved this precious
soul alive. Adam, thy words have brought great peace
to me."

ADAM—"You think so much o' me as that?"

DINAH—"Aye, Adam, not a day or a night has
passed since I knew what was in thy heart but I prayed
that God's mercy would be revealed to thee."

ADAM—"Thy prayers ha' been answered. It ha'
been revealed to me. But can full pardon be shown to
such a sinner as I ha' been?"

DINAH—"Aye, Adam, trust Him. His love is un-
failing. His mercy everlasting."

ADAM—"I do trust Him. I'm not long now for this
world, Dinah. Before I go, you'll let me say what's
in my heart?"

DINAH—"Yea, Adam."

ADAM—"You ha' filled my mind o' late, an' I ha'
grown to see what a blessed woman you ha' been to me.
If I had seen things as I ought to ha' seen them, I

should ha' known before, it was you I loved as a man should love the woman he would make his wife. I love you wi' my whole heart. If I could ha' lived would you ha' been my wife? Do you feel you could, Dinah?"

DINAH—"Yea, Adam."

ADAM—"You love me?"

DINAH—"Yea, I love thee. My heart waits on thy words and looks as a little child waits on its mother's tenderness."

ADAM—"Dinah!" (*kisses her*)

DINAH (*sobs*)—"It is too late! too late."

ADAM—"Nay, not too late. For we shall meet i' th' green fields o' heaven where there is no pain an' where th' shadow o' parting never comes."

DINAH—"Yea, I was forgetting. There we shall abide forever and forever."

ADAM—"But until you come the time o' waitin' will be long to me."

DINAH—"Nay, it will seem long only to me. For it will be no more than a day in heavenly mansions."

ADAM—"The thought o' you goes wi' me there— I'm dying fast—Do not grieve—I know that my Redeemer liveth—I ha' repented—Though your sins be as scarlet they shall be as white as snow. (*calls*) Dinah!"

DINAH (*stroking his forehead and sobbing*)—"I am here."

ADAM (*after a second struggles to his feet delirious*) —Why, mother. (*in pantomime folds her to his breast*) Seth, lad, you're surprised to see me home again? An' here's Dinah, too."

DINAH—"The God of love and peace be with him."

ADAM—"Yea, Dinah's wi' me—th' best woman i' th' world. Th' comfort o' us all. It's good to be home again. Thee'st looking rare and hearty, mother. How green th' fields are i' Hayslope, an' how fresh th' flowers smell. Seth, lad, is there plenty o' buildin' to be done i' th' village? We mun set to work wi' a will

now the war is over. There'll be no more fightin'—
Peace ha' come—yea—peace ha' come. (*recovers con-sciousness*) Dinah!" (*staggers, sinks back supported
by* SURGEON MALTBY *and* DINAH.)
    DINAH—"Adam! Adam!"

Booming of cannon.

CURTAIN.